ANGELS:

A 90-DAY DEVOTIONAL

ABOUT GOD'S MESSENGERS

Also by Christa Kinde

The Threshold Series
The Blue Door (Book One)
The Hidden Deep (Book Two)
The Broken Window (Book Three)
The Garden Gate (Book Four)

Digital Short Stories
Angels All Around
Angels in Harmony
Angels on Guard

Serial Companion Stories
Rough and Tumble
Tried and True
Sage and Song
Angel on High
Angel Unaware

Pomeroy Family Legacy Books
Pursuing Prissie

ANGELS:

A 90-DAY DEVOTIONAL

ABOUT GOD'S MESSENGERS

CHRISTA KINDE

ZONDERKIDZ

Angels: A 90-Day Devotional about God's Messengers
Copyright © 2015 by Christa Kinde

This title is also available as a Zondervan ebook. Visit www.zondervan.com/ebooks.

Requests for information should be addressed to:

Zonderkidz, 3900 Sparks Dr. SE, Grand Rapids, Michigan 49546

ISBN 978-0-310-74765-9

Cover design: Magnus Creative
Interior design: Denise Froehlich

Printed in the United States of America

15 16 17 18 19 20 /DCI/ 20 19 18 17 16 15 14 13 12 11 10 9 8 7 6 5 4 3 2 1

INTRODUCTION

> All things were created in him. He created
> everything in heaven and on earth. He created
> everything that can be seen and everything that
> can't be seen. He created kings, powers, rulers and
> authorities. All things have been created by him and
> for him.
>
> —COLOSSIANS 1:16 (NIrV)

You don't have to be a Christian to wonder about angels. They stir our curiosity and capture our imagination on universal levels. But unlike the supernatural beings of popular fiction, angels are *real*. They've been around since before the world began. And from time to time, God sends them our way.

> Divine messengers.
>
> Armed warriors.
>
> Fiery spirits.
>
> Guardian cherubim.

Angels are described in terms of light and lightning, gemstones and flames. Tales of their visits put a flutter in our hearts and a sense of awe in our souls. And why not? Their arrival has always been seen as a sign of God at work, a signal that life is about to take a dramatic turn.

Members of the heavenly host dazzled prophets in dreams, filled the air with the rush of many wings, charged into battle, and covered entire hillsides with fiery chariots. They spoke prophecies and promises. They heralded the birth of our King, and they'll accompany Him when He returns.

Ministering spirits.

Mighty ones.

Heavenly princes.

Winged seraphim.

The realm where these beings live is invisible to us. Most of the time, so are the angels themselves. So how do we know they're real? How can we be *sure* they're there? Is there proof? Simply put, we know angels are real because the Bible tells us about them. As Christians, we believe that the Scriptures are true, and I mean True with a capital T. Our Bible is God's Word, so God is the one who tells us about His amazing servants.

Throughout this devotional, I'll show you all kinds of verses that talk about angels. We'll hold Q&A sessions to help you sort fact from fiction. We'll slip into the action with Bible encounters retold—Peter's prison escape, Mary's visit from Gabriel, Daniel in the lions' den, Paul's harrowing shipwreck. For ninety days, we'll explore everything from big-picture stuff to little details. Interactive questions will keep things real and make them personal.

So lean in. Listen up. Look closer. Because there are angels all around.

CHRISTA KINDE

YE WHO SANG

A Bible Lesson

Where were you when I laid the earth's foundation? ... On what were its footings set, or who laid its cornerstone—while the morning stars sang together and all the angels shouted for joy?

—JOB 38:4–7

Neat stanzas. Majestic chords. Multiple verses. I've always loved riffling through the pages of hymn books. During my childhood, I learned so many hymns by heart. Their history interests me. The rhyming lines intrigue me. Songs are practical poetry, and four-part harmony is bliss.

In a way, hymns are teaching songs. Their authors filled them with Scripture. Many lyrics are chock full of good Bible teaching. If you pay attention to the words as you sing them, you'll learn something that's both old and new.

Christmas hymns are by far the most familiar. These carols play nonstop during the holiday season, and most folks know them well enough to hum along. But are they really listening? Consider the lyrics of "Angels from the Realms of Glory."

> *Angels from the realms of glory*
> *Wing your flight o'er all the earth;*
> *Ye who sang creation's story*
> *Now proclaim Messiah's birth.*

The wording is a little old-fashioned, but that's no problem. I can sum it up for you. Angels from heaven appeared in the skies over Bethlehem, telling the good news. And this wasn't the first time. These angels first sang when God created everything. Then they sang for their creator's birth.

How do we know angels were in the audience at the time of creation? God made it clear when He quizzed Job: "Where were you when I laid the earth's foundation? ... while the morning stars sang together and all the angels shouted for joy?" (Job 38:4–7).

"Ye who sang creation's story" refers to *in the beginning*, when stars sang and angels shouted for joy.

Dig a Little Deeper

- Do you have a favorite Christmas song? What makes it special to you? Do a little research to find all the verses. Jot down your favorite phrases. Can you tie them to Bible verses?

- Angels sang at the creation of the world. What does Luke 15:10 tell us about angels?

- Learning from lyrics certainly isn't limited to hymns. What's your current favorite Christian song? Which lines really speak to your heart? Why do they ring true?

IN THE LIONS' DEN
Meeting an Angel

Daniel said to the king, "O king, live forever!
My God sent his angel and shut the lions'
mouths, so that they have not hurt me, because
I was found innocent before Him; and also,
O King, I have done no wrong before you."

—DANIEL 6:21–22 (NKJV)

Daniel rubbed an aching hip and leaned heavily against a rough stone wall. Under the circumstances, the guards had been quite respectful in how they lowered him, but the pit was deeper than their reach. His tumble into the lions' den would leave bruises.

The darkness smelled strongly of musk, dung, and death. What little light filtered into the death trap wasn't enough to show Daniel how many executioners lay in wait. A guard with pitying eyes lifted his torch higher, then tossed it down. The wood hit stone with a sharp *clack* and a scattering of sparks that reflected in several sets of eyes.

"Use it," called the guard. "It'll hold them off for a little while."

"You have my thanks," Daniel replied. "But I'll not put my faith in something so temporary."

Shuffling farther down the wall, he fumbled around for a place to sit before his legs gave out. Then he sank to his knees and lifted his hands. Time to pick up where he left off.

"What's the old man doing?"

In startled tones, another of the guards asked, "Is he praying?"

"But ... shouldn't we stop him? He's insulting the king."

A wry voice said, "Thank you for your concern."

Daniel could practically hear the soldiers snap to attention.

Then the king called down, "Are you there, old friend?"

"O king, live forever. I am here."

"May the God you continually serve rescue you!"

With a smile, Daniel answered, "My life is in his hands."

By the king's own command, the guards closed him in. Chains rattled. Stone scraped against stone. And then there was nothing but the faint crackle of the torch's guttering flame. Slinking shadows. Deep rumbles. An echoing roar.

Was this to be his end? Covering his face, Daniel brought his fears and frustrations to God. Since his enemies couldn't discredit him, they'd redefined integrity, making Daniel's God-fearing way of life a crime. Even the king's regret couldn't save Daniel now. Daniel murmured, "My life is in your hands."

The old man prayed on, but eventually he realized that he could see light between his fingers. Slowly lowering his hands, he stared at the person who'd joined him in captivity.

Shining clothes. Calm gaze. Steady voice. "Fear not," the angel said. "You are innocent in the sight of God Most High."

Daniel managed a nod as his heaven-sent companion moved from one lion to the next, touching their muzzles and stroking their fur. Yawns replaced roars. Growls turned to sighs. And the uproar of Daniel's heart changed to peace. More confidently now, he repeated his prayer. "My life is in your hands."

Dig a Little Deeper

- Have you ever been blamed for something you didn't do? What about ridiculed for something you did? How did you deal with the sense of injustice?

- Could Daniel see the angel? How would the story change if he couldn't?

- What lessons can you learn from Daniel's example in this scenario?

"FEAR NOT"

Bible Lesson

> An angel of the Lord appeared to them,
> and the glory of the Lord shone around
> them, and they were terrified.
>
> —LUKE 2:9

The last five chapters of the book of Daniel speak about his visions, which are explained to him by the angel Gabriel. Quite the honor. Wouldn't you like to be in Daniel's sandals? Don't be so sure. This incident was not like his first angelic encounter.

> As he came near the place where I was standing, I was terrified and fell prostrate.
>
> —DANIEL 8:17

> While he was speaking to me, I was in a deep sleep, with my face to the ground.
>
> —DANIEL 8:18

> I had no strength left, my face turned deathly pale and I was helpless.
>
> —DANIEL 10:8

> As I listened to him, I fell into a deep sleep, my face to the ground.
>
> —DANIEL 10:9

I bowed with my face toward the ground and was speechless.
—DANIEL 10:15

I said ... "I am overcome with anguish because of the vision, my lord, and I feel very weak."
—DANIEL 10:16

My strength is gone and I can hardly breathe.
—DANIEL 10:17

No wonder "fear not" seems to be at the start of every angelic conversation. The presence of one angel was enough to turn Daniel's knees to jelly, steal the breath from his lungs, and send him toppling to the floor in a dead faint. Your first inclination might be, "What a wimp." But don't be hasty. Consider what this guy had already done. Daniel stood before kings, against liars, and for his beliefs. He had real courage, which leads to one certain conclusion.

Yep. Angels can be just that scary. There's no downplaying their awe-factor. No one can stand in the presence of God—except angels. And those who've met angels have met the floor. Usually at great speed.

Dig a Little Deeper

- Name some of the things that scare you. What's the difference between fear and awe?

- What gives you moments of awe? What tugs at your sense of wonder? How does your soul respond—tears, gratitude, creativity, worship, something else?

- Have you ever wanted to meet an angel? Does Daniel's experience give you second thoughts?

Q. WILL CHRISTIANS BECOME ANGELS IN HEAVEN?

Q&A

At the resurrection people ... will
be like the angels in heaven.

—MATTHEW 22:30

No. People don't sprout wings and put on a halo after they die. The Bible is clear that humans and angels are distinct from each other. So what's the difference? Let's cover a few basics.

What is an angel? Angels are supernatural beings who primarily exist as spirits (see Heb. 1:14). From various Bible passages, we catch a glimpse of who they are—powerful, intelligent, and capable of choice. They have emotions and individuality. They were created by God: "Praise him, all his angels ... for at his command they were created" (Ps. 148:2, 5). And they serve God: "You mighty ones who do his bidding" (Ps. 103:20).

When were angels created? From Job 38:4–7, we learn that angels watched God create the world. "Where were you when I laid the earth's foundation? ... On what were its footings set, or who laid its cornerstone—while the morning stars sang together and all the angels shouted for joy?" They were formed before humans, but we don't know for certain how long before us that God made them.

Where do angels live? Angels have their home in the heavens. We know Gabriel stands in God's presence (see Luke 1:19), and Jesus said, "angels in heaven always see the face of my Father in heaven" (Matt. 18:10). They are often here on earth, and some are entrusted with watching over certain groups of people.

How are angels different than we are? One way in which we're different from angels is that they cannot be forgiven. "God did not spare angels when they sinned, but sent them to hell, putting them in chains of darkness to be held for judgment" (2 Peter 2:4). Their fallen won't be saved, but Jesus made it possible for our sins to be cancelled. "In him we have redemption through his blood, the forgiveness of sins, in accordance with the riches of God's grace" (Eph. 1:7).

How will we be like the angels? Believers will have a place in heaven. Like the angels, we'll stand before God's throne and be able to see Jesus face-to-face. Sin and sorrow will end. We'll worship the Lord with all that we are. Our faith will become sight. Forevermore.

Someday, Christians will join God and His angels in heaven, but we won't *become* angels.

Dig a Little Deeper

- What comes to mind when you hear the word *angelic*?
- Why do you suppose people are so curious about angels? What about them interests you?
- What are you looking forward to about heaven? Are there questions you're saving up for God?

FIRST COME, FIRST SERVED

A Bible Lesson

For an angel went down at a certain time into the pool and stirred up the water; then whoever stepped in first, after the stirring of the water, was made well of whatever disease he had.

—JOHN 5:4 (NKJV)

Did you ever wonder about the story of the angel who stirred the water? In Jesus' day, sick people camped out around the pool at Bethesda, vying for their chance at a miracle. According to eyewitness accounts, an angel sometimes visited the pool. Sure, he was invisible, but you knew he was there because the water reacted to his presence—swishing, swirling, bubbling up. And if you were lucky enough to reach the moving water first, you'd be healed.

On the one, hand, wow! What a show of divine power!

But on the other hand, ouch! All those people, and only *one* shot at a clean bill of health. I somehow doubt the prize always went to the neediest or most patient. Wouldn't people push and shove? Why would God ask people to claw past one another, wrestling for their chance at his healing touch? And it raises tough questions. If God could heal one, why not everyone? Why is one spared while others continue to suffer? Suddenly God seems kind of stingy.

But *stingy* isn't part of God's character, so what was going on here?

Let's turn it around and consider the situation from the angel's perspective. As a faithful servant, he waited in the midst of those gathered to see what God would do. He stood ready to bestow one precious miracle. Not because God is stingy. Far from it. Our Father in heaven didn't have to heal *anyone*.

When the time was exactly right, God gave the command, and the angel stirred the water. And he watched to see who was first to reach the water. Because that would be the signal he'd been waiting for. It's how he knew who God wanted him to heal. And so one desperate person's faith was rewarded. Because God is generous.

Dig a Little Deeper

- Do you know someone who's been miraculously healed? How was their life changed? How did it affect their faith?

- Do you know someone who *didn't* get the miracle they prayed for? What was the outcome of their story? How did their struggle touch those around them?

- Read 2 Corinthians 12:1–10. What was Paul's attitude toward his ongoing trouble? Do you deal with something challenging on a daily basis? How do you face it?

JOSEPH THE DREAMER
Meeting an Angel

> An angel of the Lord appeared to him in a
> dream. The angel said, "Joseph, son of David,
> don't be afraid to take Mary home as your wife.
> The baby inside her is from the Holy Spirit."
> —MATTHEW 1:20 (NIRV)

Once was enough. After his family laughed and called him Joseph the Dreamer, he kept quiet about the visions. The last thing he and Mary needed was more fuel for the whispers that spread like wildfire through their families, to the neighbors, and across Nazareth. They assumed the worst.

"For shame! Will he divorce her?"

"I would. He can do better."

Head down. Mouth shut. Back straight. Joseph adjusted his grip on his mallet and focused on connecting cleanly with his chisel. He had work to do. God had given him a family to provide for. One he'd do anything to protect. Even at the cost of his reputation.

"How can he overlook her sin?"

"It must be his child. Why else would he keep her?"

The accusations were unjust. The pity unwanted. But if no one else ever knew the full truth, he and Mary had one thing in common. A shining messenger had visited each of them. Gabriel—*the* Gabriel—had come down from heaven and ruined all their plans with his "good news."

"She always seemed like a sweet girl."

"Poor Joseph."

Joseph could have defended himself, but not without shaming Mary. Mary could have explained, but not without betraying a precious secret. This whole situation was beyond Joseph's grasp. Impossible in every way. And yet he believed the angel whose voice still rang in his ears. The Messiah was coming.

In the midst of the scandal and confusion, one thought steadied Joseph. Deep in his heart, he could understand heaven's choice. He'd always believed Mary was wonderful. It came as no surprise that God himself agreed.

Dig a Little Deeper

- Would you have trouble keeping a secret if an angel visited you?
- What's the harm in rumors and gossip?
- What do you admire in Joseph? Why?

Q. What's a Halo?

Q&A

His appearance was like lightning, and
his clothes were white as snow.

—Matthew 28:3

The most iconic feature of angels in art has to be the halo. Those golden circlets let us know that an angel *is* an angel. That's why cherub choirs at Christmastime are decked out with tinsel headbands or pipe cleaner approximations. Does this mean real angels sport levitating circlets? Doubtful.

While the halo is common in religious art, it's just a symbol. This "nimbus" or cloud of light marks a person as special. You will find floating disks of light over the portraits of apostles and saints to show that they're holy, set apart, admired. And in the case of Jesus, divine.

Halos are sometimes called windows into heaven, so it's only natural that people *from* heaven would be crowned by its light. The Bible doesn't use the word *halo,* but both David and the writer of Hebrews use the phrase *crowned with glory and honor* (see Ps. 8:5; Heb. 2:7, 9). If nothing else, the halo is an artistic reminder that God's angels have a shine all their own. "Suddenly two men in clothes that gleamed like lightning stood beside them" (Luke 24:4). Both an angel's clothes and his face were bright enough to set him apart ... and send men and women to their knees.

Dig a Little Deeper

- How is the coming of the Holy Spirit described in Acts 2:1–3?
- What gift do we receive from the God who said, "Let light shine out of darkness," according to 2 Corinthians 4:6? Does that describe you?
- Read Matthew 5:13–16. Could this be *your* "halo"?

DAY 8

God Came Down
A Bible Lesson

He was in the assembly in the wilderness, with
the angel who spoke to him on Mount Sinai.

—Acts 7:38

Not long after sunrise, a tremor startled the children of God. The earth moved underfoot, and they emerged from their tents to look at the mountain. Whispers scattered through the encampment, and mothers did their best to calm frightened children. Strange clouds were gathering and twisting around the peak.

Tension thickened the air, and flickering light accompanied the growl of thunder. The earth quaked, sending all God's people to their knees. And from amid the unnatural storm came a trumpet blast. Smoke billowed up, hiding the entire mountain from view, and fire fell from heaven. Word passed quickly through the tribes. Moses would climb Mount Sinai. And there he would meet with God (see Ex. 19).

You came down on Mount Sinai; you spoke to them
from heaven. You gave them regulations and laws that
are just and right, and decrees and commands that
are good.

—Nehemiah 9:13

The mountains quaked before the LORD, the One of Sinai, before the LORD, the God of Israel.

—JUDGES 5:5

The earth shook, the heavens poured down rain, before God, the One of Sinai, before God, the God of Israel.

—PSALM 68:8

According to the Bible, an angel had a part in the giving of the Law to Moses. Flickering like lightning. Filling the air with trumpet blasts. For a while, at the top of the mountain, heaven touched earth. Amid shining smoke, holy fire, and rumbling noise, Moses met with God. Luke says, "And he received living words to pass on to us" (Acts 7:38). And the pastor who wrote the book of Hebrews warned followers of God to pay special attention to "the message spoken through angels" (Heb. 2:1–3).

Dig a Little Deeper

- How would you have reacted to the supernatural display of power at Mount Sinai?
- What happened to Moses because he spent so much time in God's presence, according to Exodus 34:29–30?
- Read Psalm 17:15. What does David say he cannot wait to see?

IN THE PRESENCE OF GOD

Meeting an Angel

> But the angel said to him: "Do not be afraid,
> Zechariah; your prayer has been heard."
> —LUKE 1:13

Jerusalem buzzed with the business of worship. It was the time of year when priests from the order of Abijah served God in the temple, and Zechariah was counted among them. Spotless linen. Swaying tassels. Measured steps. A priest could spend his whole life in service and never set foot beyond the outer court-yard where he stoked the fires, slaughtered animals, and offered prayers. Decades of dedication had come to a high point that morning when the lots were cast, and Zechariah was chosen to enter the Holy Place. Shallow breaths. Lowered gaze. Nearly there.

Zechariah approached the heavy veil that hid the inner rooms from view. Purple and blue, scarlet and white—only those from the tribe of Levi were permitted to see what lay beyond these ornately embroidered folds. He had prepared for this moment. Conscience clear. Heart humbled. Pulse racing. Uncomfortably conscious of the soft jingle of bells at his ankles, Zechariah took a shaky gulp of air and stepped into the presence of God.

Resisting the urge to tiptoe across the chamber, he approached the altar of incense and added fresh coals taken from the large altar in the courtyard. Slow motion. Reverent silence. Simple duties. Soon, the rich smell of worship bathed his senses—sweet spices and frankincense. He closed his eyes and savored the sacred aroma. To calm his reeling mind for prayer, the old priest dredged up a psalm, silently rehearsing its prayer. *Hear us, O Shepherd of Israel, you who lead Joseph like a flock; you who sit enthroned between the cherubim, shine forth.*

Those outside the veil would add their prayers to this offering, but this evening, Zechariah stood before God on behalf of his people. His flock. His children. In an instant, Zechariah's thoughts flew to home and to Elizabeth. His wife never complained, but she would have liked to give him a child. Empty arms. Aching heart. Past hope. But this was neither the time nor the place to be dwelling on such things.

Opening his eyes, he gasped and leapt backward with an abrupt jangle of bells. A man robed in white stood to the right of the golden altar. Shining face. Fearsome gaze. Bringing judgment? Zechariah gripped his chest and fumbled for an apology, but the angel said, "Do not be afraid, Zechariah; your prayer has been heard. Your wife Elizabeth will bear you a son."

Dig a Little Deeper

- Do the answers to your prayers always come about in the way you expect? Share a time when God surprised you.

- Zechariah's whole life is summed up in Luke 1:6. If you could sum yourself up in a few words, which ones would you use? What's your reputation? How do you want to be remembered?

- All Zechariah's bottled up thoughts poured out as a song (see Luke 1:67–80). What predictions did the song hold? What promises?

EXPECTANT PARENTS

A Bible Lesson

For to us a child is born, to us a son is given.

—ISAIAH 9:6

The word of the Lord came to many people, for many reasons. Promises. Prophecies. Commands. Comfort. One message that he gave repeatedly was good news of a special variety. God frequently used his angels to deliver baby announcements!

Ishmael's mother: "You are now pregnant and you will give birth to a son" (Gen. 16:11).

Isaac's father: "I will surely return to you about this time next year, and Sarah your wife will have a son" (Gen. 18:10).

Samson's mother: "You are barren and childless, but you are going to become pregnant and give birth to a son" (Judg. 13:3).

John's father: "Do not be afraid, Zechariah; your prayer has been heard. Your wife Elizabeth will bear you a son, and you are to call him John" (Luke 1:13).

Jesus' mother: "Do not be afraid, Mary, you have found favor with God. You will conceive and give birth to a son, and you are to call him Jesus" (Luke 1:30–31).

Jesus' adoptive father: "Joseph son of David, do not be afraid to take Mary home as your wife, because what is conceived in her is from the Holy Spirit" (Matt. 1:20).

Dig a Little Deeper

- Read Psalm 127:3. Why might children be considered a gift, a blessing, or even a treasure?
- How can you treat life as precious?
- According to Luke 3:22, how did God feel about His Son, Jesus Christ?

YOUR SON, YOUR ONLY SON

Meeting an Angel

But the angel of the LORD called out to him
from heaven, "Abraham! Abraham!"
—GENESIS 22:11

Wood for the offering. Stone for the altar. Abraham studied the knife and fought the urge to throw it off the mountain. He didn't understand. Couldn't. Why would God give him a son to love, then call for his blood upon an altar?

God had set before Abraham a terrible choice, but it was one he couldn't bring himself to undo. If God asked for Isaac, Abraham would trust the boy into the Lord's keeping. Even now, Abraham didn't know if he could slay his own child, but he would take this journey one step at a time. Just as he had always done. For this was faith.

The climb onto Mount Moriah wasn't easy for a man of his years. Every time his son helped him along a difficult patch, Abraham's grief deepened.

"Father?"

"Yes, my son?"

"We have wood and fire, but where is the lamb?"

Abraham answered, "God will provide a lamb, my son."

God directed them to the place, and Abraham set stone upon stone, building an altar. The solemn expression on Isaac's face cut him deeply. Tears blurred old eyes as he arranged the wood. Setting aside the knife, Abraham showed Isaac the rope and said, "Come here, my son."

And like a lamb, Isaac stepped forward.

By the time Abraham set the boy on top of the wood, they were both crying. Pleas for trust. Promises of love. And faith enough to steel himself to obey the one true God. Abraham lifted his hand and whispered good-bye.

When the angel called Abraham's name, the blade slipped from numb fingers. Choking on a ragged sob, Abraham answered, "Here I am."

"Do not lay a hand on the boy," said the angel. "Do not do anything to him. Now I know that you fear God, because you have not withheld from me your son, your only son."

And the God he loved and feared provided a better sacrifice.

For God so loved the world that he gave his one and only Son.

—JOHN 3:16

Dig a Little Deeper

- Why did God stop Abraham? Why didn't God step in when His own son was sacrificed?

- Because of his obedience, what promise did God make to Abraham in Genesis 22:18?

- Though God doesn't require altar sacrifices anymore, someday He may ask you to make a tough sacrifice. Will your faith be strong enough to say yes?

Stars in the Daytime
A Bible Lesson

In speaking of the angels he says, "He makes his
angels spirits, and his servants flames of fire."

—Hebrews 1:7

The realm of angels is invisible to humans, but that doesn't
mean it doesn't exist. God has hidden them from view, like
stars in the daytime. We have the sun—His Son—which is all we
need for light and life. Angels shine unseen. But they're as real as
you and I, and we'll see them clearly one day.

By faith we understand that the universe was formed at
God's command, so that what is seen was not made
out of what was visible.

—Hebrews 11:3

For in him all things were created: things in heaven
and on earth, visible and invisible, whether thrones or
powers or rulers or authorities.

—Colossians 1:16

Grace and peace to you from him who is, and who
was, and who is to come, and from the seven spirits
before his throne.

—Revelation 1:4

Angels live with God in a spiritual realm (see Zech. 6:5), hidden by His light (see 1 Tim. 6:16), and they're compared to lightning (see Dan. 10:6) and flames of fire (see Heb. 1:7), which flicker briefly before our eyes. They're also compared to the wind (see Ps. 35:5), which cannot be seen, but is definitely felt. Much like God himself, whose Spirit is compared to the wind in John 3:8. "The wind blows wherever it pleases. You hear its sound, but you cannot tell where it comes from or where it is going. So it is with everyone born of the Spirit."

> Ever since the world was created it has been possible to see the qualities of God that are not seen. I'm talking about his eternal power and about the fact that he is God. Those things can be seen in what he has made.
>
> —ROMANS 1:20 (NIrV)

Dig a Little Deeper

- There are two famous sayings. "Out of sight, out of mind." And then, "absence makes the heart grow fonder." Which describes you more?

- Name some invisible things that you regularly rely on. Do you have to see things to believe in them?

- Read the famous definition of faith in the first two verses of Hebrews 11. When have you taken a leap of faith?

Q. How many angels can dance on the head of a pin?

Q&A

Can his forces be numbered?
—Job 25:3

The angels question has been around since medieval times, and it has inspired its fair share of drama. It's one part riddle, one part trick question. And those who first asked this question *knew* there was no answer. Another word-trap is this stumper: Can God create a stone that's too heavy for Him to lift? Believe it or not, there are people who think that a Christian's inability to give sensible answers to questions like these means that God and His angels don't exist. Talk about a leap of illogic!

These questions and others like them are classic attempts at giving someone the runaround. In fact, that dancing angels question is now used as a metaphor for pointless arguments. Questions like that are a waste of time. So what's a better question?

Q. Are there angels?
A. Yes.

Q. How many?
A. Lots.

Q. Can you be more specific?
A. Only as specific as Scripture gets. Take a look at these verses:

Suddenly there was with the angel a multitude of the heavenly host praising God.

—LUKE 2:13 (NKJV)

Then I looked and heard the voice of many angels, numbering thousands upon thousands, and ten thousand times ten thousand.

—REVELATION 5:11

You have come to thousands upon thousands of angels in joyful assembly.

—HEBREWS 12:22

Grab a calculator and tally up all those *thousands* and *upons*. Several zeros later, you'll find yourself in the hundreds of millions. Now consider this! Most of the New Testament was written in Greek, and at that time, their word for the largest number was *ten thousand*. So the people who wrote about the heavenly host pulled the biggest number they knew, then told us to multiply it.

Are there millions, billions, trillions? Only God knows. But we do know that those who caught a glimpse of heaven's angels ended up with boggled minds. Words failed. Numbers fell short. It's beyond our understanding … beyond our imagining … and entirely real.

Dig a Little Deeper

- How do you deal with questions about your faith that are hard to answer?
- God asked Abraham to number the stars. He challenged Job to measure how far the east is from the west. And we know that every snowflake that's ever fallen is as unique as the whorls of every person's fingerprint. Knowing that creation is filled with so many countless things, are you amazed to know that you matter?
- What place would you like to have in God's vast plans?

DESTROYING ANGEL

Meeting an Angel

> Satan rose up against Israel and incited
> David to take a census of Israel.
>
> —1 CHRONICLES 21:1

Two scouts came running to meet David and his men, who drew to a halt on the dusty road. "Well?" asked the king. "Are we close?"

"Very." One of the men pointed into the valley. "These vineyards and fields belong to Araunah the Jebusite. We should be able to see his threshing floor from here."

Everyone looked toward the opposite rise, and several gasped. Murmurs rippled through the king's personal guard. "Am I seeing things?

"What *is* that?"

"It's an *angel*!"

David's voice was hollow, but it still cut across the whispers. "That's our destination. Let's go."

They left the road, splitting ranks as they filed through long rows of grape vines. David glanced up when the captain of his guard fell in step beside him. "News?"

"My men asked for more than directions. Looks like the surrounding cities are also in mourning."

The king winced. "This is all my fault."

When the prophet Gad came to confront David's sin, he offered the king an impossible choice—three years of famine, three months of flight, or three days of plague *and* the sword of the Lord. Cut to the heart, David chose the latter, throwing himself into the Lord's hands. Surely, God's mercy was better than his foolishness.

"Did I make the right choice?"

"To trust God? Yes."

"Was there more?" He searched his companion's face. "How bad is it?"

His captain kept his voice low. "From Dan to Beersheba, no less than seventy thousand."

David groaned. "I was a fool to number our men. Now I get to tally the dead."

The group didn't get much farther before two of his guards signaled urgently. They'd found Araunah himself. The man and his four sons had cowered in a ditch below the threshing floor.

"… without warning, like a rush of wind. And when we turned, he was there. A shining warrior with a sword!" The pale-faced farmer was speaking quickly. "We've been here since, for fear of his wrath. Who can stand before the Lord?"

David stepped forward. "God has commanded me to build an altar here. Will you consent?"

"Take it! Take it and do whatever you want!" The farmer bowed low. "All you need. Oxen for the offering. Threshing sledges for wood. Even wheat for the grain offering. I'll gladly give it all!"

Clasping the man's hands, David warmly answered, *"Thank you*. But I'm not here to take another thing from God's people. I'll pay the full price for what's needed."

The man glanced from face to face. "If that's what you want."

"I insist." David's gaze darted to the looming angel whose bare blade flashed in the sun. The price for his sin was staggering. "Far be it from me to bring a sacrifice that cost me nothing."

David built an altar to the LORD there and sacrificed burnt offerings and fellowship offerings. He called on the LORD, and the LORD answered him with fire from heaven on the altar of burnt offering. Then the LORD spoke to the angel, and he put his sword back into its sheath.

—1 CHRONICLES 21:26–27

Dig a Little Deeper

- David was called a man after God's own heart. Does that mean he was perfect?
- Have you ever made a major blunder? How did you feel afterward?
- David refused to bring an offering that cost him nothing, so he paid for Araunah's land. What does making a sacrifice mean for us?

ENTHRONED BETWEEN THE CHERUBIM

A Bible Lesson

Give ear, O Shepherd of Israel, You who
lead Joseph like a flock; You who dwell
between the cherubim, shine forth!
—PSALM 80:1 (NKJV)

The priest entered the Holy Place of the temple with hot coals and a heady mixture of spices, ready to tend to the altar of incense. "Every morning and evening they present burnt offerings and fragrant incense to the LORD" (2 Chron. 13:11). This faithful, old priest had prepared his heart for his sacred duty.

Beyond a second curtain stood the famous ark of the covenant. "The priests then brought the ark of the LORD's covenant to its place in the inner sanctuary of the temple, the Most Holy Place, and put it beneath the wings of the cherubim" (1 Kings 8:6). Only the High Priest could pass beyond that line and gaze upon the ark.

The sculptures of twin angels spread their wings over a golden seat, according to the Lord's own instruction (see Ex. 25:18–22). So throughout the Old Testament, the God of Israel is called the one "enthroned between the cherubim."

So the people sent to Shiloh, that they might bring from there the ark of the covenant of the LORD of hosts, who dwells *between* the cherubim.

—1 SAMUEL 4:4 (NKJV)

Hezekiah prayed before the LORD, and said: "O Lord God of Israel, the One who dwells *between* the cherubim, You are God, You alone, of all the kingdoms of the earth.

—2 KINGS 19:15 (NKJV)

David and all Israel went to … bring up from there the ark of God the LORD, who is enthroned between the cherubim.

—1 CHRONICLES 13:6

He sits enthroned between the cherubim, let the earth shake.

—PSALM 99:1

It would be easy to assume that the Most Holy Place was God's throne room, but this glorious, golden room—veiled from prying eyes, filled with priceless treasures, saturated by the incense of generations of prayers—was merely His footstool (see 1 Chron. 28:2).

Heaven is my throne, and the earth is my footstool.

—ISAIAH 66:1

Exalt the LORD our God and worship at his footstool; he is holy.

—PSALM 99:5

> Let us go to his dwelling place, let us worship at his footstool.
>
> —Psalm 132:7

In this temple where God was honored, two cherubim reminded the priests that they were not alone in their worship. They joined an invisible multitude. Angels surround God's throne in heaven, "thousands upon thousands, and ten thousand times ten thousand," continuously tell of His glory (Rev. 5:11). The visible *and* the invisible praise Him.

Dig a Little Deeper

- Read the description of heaven's throne in Revelation 4. Which part do you like best—the door that leads into heaven, the encircling rainbow, the brilliant flashes of light, or the crystal sea?

- How should we approach God's throne according to Hebrews 4:16?

- If God is King, what is our role in His kingdom?

Nothing Is Impossible
Meeting an Angel

God sent the angel Gabriel to
Nazareth, a town in Galilee.
—LUKE 1:26

Mary hadn't jumped so high since the time she'd found a mouse in their grain bin. Hands over her mouth, she held in a scream that would have brought the family running. A man. And what a man! Backing into the corner, Mary leaned against the wall.

"Greetings, you who are highly favored. The Lord is with you."

Impossible.

Mary knew the Scriptures. She'd been told about angels since she was tiny. But angels belonged in the grandeur of the temple, or at least in a place of honor in the synagogue. What was one doing here, in a simple home?

But then a thought occurred to her. How many generations had passed since God's angel had visited Daniel? Yet he fit the description. White robes. Golden sash. Mary's cheeks flushed, then paled. Could this be him? The one from the stories?

"I am Gabriel, and I have been sent to speak to you."

Impossible.

Mary wavered. The same Gabriel? Here?

"Do not be afraid, Mary, you have found favor with God."

Gabriel's next words left her reeling, for he spoke of the great Messiah. Every generation watched for him, hoped for him. The Messiah would save them. His reign would bring peace to Israel. Every daughter of Judah—especially those from the line of David—hoped that their son would become a king. But the angel's message told a different story than the one Mary knew. Yes, the Messiah would come as a man, but He would be the Son of God. And she would be His mother.

"How?"

His answer set her heart at ease.

"Nothing is impossible with God."

Dig a Little Deeper

- Mary grew up with stories like Noah's ark and Daniel in the lion's den, the same as you and me. Do you think this made Gabriel's arrival harder or easier to believe for Mary?

- God uses Gabriel to set his plan in motion on earth. How long had it been in the works, according to 1 Corinthians 2:7?

- Read Luke 1:46–55. What was Mary's response to being chosen by God?

Q. WHY DO WE SAY THAT ANGELS HAVE WINGS?

Q&A

> He mounted the cherubim and flew; he
> soared on the wings of the wind.
>
> —PSALM 18:10

The short answer: that's how the Bible describes some of them. While not all angels are described as having wings, many did. Here, I'll show you. Let's start with Isaiah's vision of heaven, where he spotted several seraphim.

> Above him were seraphim, each with six wings: With
> two wings they covered their faces, with two they cov-
> ered their feet, and with two they were flying.
>
> —ISAIAH 6:2

Of course, not all angels have six wings. In Exodus, we get a detailed description of the ark of the covenant, which was built according to God's instructions. The Israelite craftsmen took great care in creating a pair of cherubim for the mercy seat on the ark of the covenant. Each cherub had two wings.

> Then he made two cherubim out of hammered gold at
> the ends of the cover. He made one cherub on one
> end and the second cherub on the other; at the two
> ends he made them of one piece with the cover. The

cherubim had their wings spread upward, overshad-
owing the cover with them. The cherubim faced each
other, looking toward the cover.

—EXODUS 37:7–9

We also have a description from Solomon's temple, where a
matched set of cherubim stood guard. These fellas were 15 feet
tall, carved from olive wood, and overlaid with gold.

He placed the cherubim inside the innermost room of
the temple, with their wings spread out. The wing of
one cherub touched one wall, while the wing of the
other touched the other wall, and their wings touched
each other in the middle of the room.

—1 KINGS 6:27

And then there were the walls and doors of the sanctuary.
The craftsmen beautified them with intricate carvings based on
the same angelic design. Cherubim figured prominently into
these decorations, and they were overlaid with even more hammered gold.

On the walls all around the temple, in both the inner
and outer rooms, he carved cherubim, palm trees and
open flowers.

—1 KINGS 6:29

Dig a Little Deeper

- Read Psalm 61:4. What did David long for? What do you think
  that would be like?
- When or where do you feel the safest?
- Who offers protection and comfort like the wings of a bird? What
  blessing do we find in Ruth 2:12 and Psalm 91:4?

A STONE FOR A PILLOW

Meeting an Angel

> In a dream he saw a stairway standing on the earth. Its top reached to heaven. The angels of God were going up and coming down on it.
>
> —GENESIS 28:12 (NIrV)

Jacob put as much distance between himself and Beersheba as he could before sunset. Near Luz, he looked back in the direction of his father's lands. No sign of pursuit on the horizon. But there wouldn't be. Mother had promised. Father would hold Esau back.

"You were a fool, brother," Jacob muttered. Maybe it was cowardly to speak from a safe distance, but Jacob had things to say. A little louder, he announced, "I'm not running from you. This has always been the plan. You were impatient, but *I* can see farther than my appetite."

His twin brother was a strong man, a great hunter, and their father's pride, but that didn't make Esau better. Whether it was a bowl of stew or a beautiful woman, Esau grabbed up whatever he wanted. And for once, he would taste the consequences of impatience.

After holding his tongue for so many years, Jacob relished this one-sided rant against Esau. "You sold your birthright! Your inheritance has passed to me! And you cannot undo what I've done!"

Well, there was one way. But Esau wouldn't resort to murder while their father was alive. Probably. That's why Mother had

44

helped Jacob arrange a journey to Haran. Isaac had begged Esau not to take Canaanite wives, without success. But Jacob knew when to listen. "I'll follow in Father's footsteps and take a wife from among our kinsmen. Our parents will bless my choice."

Isaac's parting words still rang in Jacob's ears: "May the Mighty God bless you. May he give you children. May he make your family larger until you become a community of nations. May he give you and your children after you the blessing he gave to Abraham" (Gen. 28:3–4, NIrV).

Making do with a stone for a pillow, Jacob lay back and gazed at the stars. They blazed in the sky, a glittering reminder of his grandfather's covenant. One day, his own descendants would be as countless. So Jacob would barter for a better bride. One to please the God of Abraham and Isaac.

Then a dream swept him into the sky, and he hung helpless before a glittering multitude. An impossible path stretched from the earth below into the heavens above. Brilliant creatures passed one another, some traveling up, others headed down. But their dazzling presence was nothing compared to the voice that filled Jacob's mind: "I am the LORD. I am the God of your grandfather Abraham and the God of Isaac. I will give you and your children after you the land you are lying on" (Gen. 28:13, NIrV)

Angels witnessed the renewal of a promise. One that first belonged to Abraham and to Isaac. One that boggled the mind and humbled the heart. One that would mean hope and a home for generations.

Dig a Little Deeper

- Read Genesis 28:14–15. Does God's promise to Abraham, Isaac, and Jacob have any effect on us?
- What did Jacob think when he awoke from his dream (see Gen. 28:16–19)?
- What did Jesus say in John 1:51? How is this similar to Jacob's experience?

Q. DO ANGELS LIVE ON CLOUD NINE?

Q&A

> For I tell you that their angels in heaven always see the face of my Father in heaven.
>
> —MATTHEW 18:10

Artists often depict angels sitting high up in the clouds, but no, angels don't live on the fabled "cloud nine." It's believed this phrase refers to big, puffy cumulonimbus clouds. They were ninth of the ten cloud types listed in the 1896 edition of the *International Cloud Atlas.*

Maybe one of the reasons people link clouds and heaven is because of Jesus' ascension. When He returned to heaven, the disciples watched Him rise high into the sky, until a cloud hid Him from view. What's more, two angels appeared and told the disciples that Jesus would come back in the same way they saw Him go into heaven (see Acts 1:9–11). Jesus and His angels will be coming in the sky, so cloud watching could be considered a natural pastime for believers:

> And then all the peoples of the earth will mourn when they see the Son of Man coming on the clouds of heaven, with power and great glory.
>
> —MATTHEW 24:30

We who are still alive and are left will be caught up together with them in the clouds to meet the Lord in the air. And so we will be with the Lord forever.

—1 Thessalonians 4:17

"Look, he is coming with the clouds," and "every eye will see him" ... So shall it be! Amen.

—Revelation 1:7

Angels are the hosts of heaven, the population and citizens of an invisible realm. Theirs is a heavenly country (see Heb. 11:16), sometimes called the "third heaven," (2 Cor. 12:2), the holy city (see Rev. 21:2), and Paradise (see 2 Cor. 12:4). When Jesus returns for us, heaven will be our home too.

Dig a Little Deeper

- What do you think about when you look into the clouds?
- Are you looking forward to Jesus' return? What will change when He comes?
- Do you think you'll still have to walk by faith once you can see God, heaven, and angels? Are faith and faithfulness the same thing?

WHILE SHEPHERDS WATCHED

Meeting an Angel

> Suddenly a great company of the heavenly
> host appeared with the angel.
>
> —LUKE 2:13

The star was pretty enough. A little piece of heaven. A speck of glory. Like what King David said in the days when he was a shepherd. How the stars showed off. Heavens declaring. Skies shouting.

No one could figure how he got so close without scaring the sheep. But there he came, calm as you please, right up to where the shepherds were sitting. At first, they thought they were seeing things. Wasn't he shining like a star himself? But one guy whistled sharp, and the rest of them came running. Didn't take long for the lot of them to get behind the tallest shepherd. They made him their shield, and that must have made him their spokesman. Because the shining one looked him right in the eye. And just like that, the shepherd lowered his staff. Scared as he was, he knew the stories as well as anyone.

An angel.

Most of the shepherds were crouched and cowering. The tall one almost keeled over himself on account of forgetting how to breathe. But he couldn't look away. The angel was just like the stories always said, lightning-bright. And when he spoke, his voice rang clear. Not a man on that hillside could have missed his words.

"Fear not! I have good news that will bring great joy to all people! Today, in the town of David, a Savior has been born. He is Christ the Lord."

Before long, the shepherds sorted out what the angel must mean. One man whispered, "Messiah."

Others repeated it and asked, "Here? In Bethlehem?"

The angel gave directions. They'd know it was the Messiah because He'd be tucked into a manger. Then more angels appeared, and the shepherds dropped like stones. One angel was flustering enough, but he was a speck of glory compared to his crew. It was like God pulled aside the night sky like a tent flap so they could look right through into heaven. No one could have counted the dazzling host. And their words rang in the shepherds' ears.

"Glory to God in the highest!"

They were gone so quickly that the shepherds thought they'd imagined the whole thing. But, together, they headed to Bethlehem to see for themselves. And they found the Messiah, just like the angels had said. A speck of glory, swaddled snugly in the straw of a manger.

Dig a Little Deeper

- What Bible verses or Bible stories come to mind when you see the stars?
- Why do you think God brought news of His Son's birth to shepherds?
- How would you tell the story from the point of view of the angels?

Q. ARE THERE DIFFERENT KINDS OF ANGELS?

Q&A

> Then I saw another mighty angel coming down
> from heaven. He was robed in a cloud, with
> a rainbow above his head; his face was like
> the sun, and his legs were like fiery pillars.
>
> —REVELATION 10:1

Although we only have the names for two specific orders of angels, the Bible describes several unusual creatures and hints at different ranks and roles. These beings are called the hosts of heaven or starry host (see Neh. 9:6), thrones and dominions (see Col. 1:16), guardians (see Ps. 91:11–12, Dan 12:1), warriors (see Josh. 5:13–15, Rev. 12:7), angels and authorities (see 1 Pet. 3:22), and ministering spirits (see Heb. 1:14). The two orders that the Bible names are the cherubim (the singular is cherub) and the seraphim (the singular is seraph).

Cherubim

> After he drove the man out, he placed on the east side
> of the Garden of Eden cherubim and a flaming sword
> flashing back and forth to guard the way to the tree
> of life.
>
> —GENESIS 3:24

Seraphim

Above him were seraphim, each with six wings: With two wings they covered their faces, with two they covered their feet, and with two they were flying.

—ISAIAH 6:2

There are more verses about strange and beautiful heavenly beings. Have you ever noticed these passages in your Bible?

Living Creatures

And in the fire was what looked like four living creatures. In appearance their form was human, but each of them had four faces and four wings.

—EZEKIEL 1:5–6

Wheels within Wheels

This was the appearance and structure of the wheels: They sparkled like topaz ... Each appeared to be made like a wheel intersecting a wheel ... Their rims were high and awesome, and all four rims were full of eyes all around.

—EZEKIEL 1:16–18

Dig a Little Deeper

- Do all angels fit our usual mental image of beautiful winged people? How do you think you would react to meeting one of these other strange creatures?
- Where else do you see variety in God's creation?
- How does this change your idea of what heaven will be like?

The Righteous Centurion

Meeting an Angel

He distinctly saw an angel of God.
—Acts 10:3

He was an outsider and always would be. As a representative of the occupying government, Cornelius was looked on with a mixture of suspicion and fear. But this didn't stop him from hearing their stories. Nor from believing them.

Cornelius had come to faith long ago, and in an effort to please the God of Israel, he'd quietly adopted several of their customs. Maybe he would never find favor in the sight of these people, but perhaps he could find favor in the eyes of the one true God. Gifts for the poor. Fairness in his dealings. Kindness where it was needed. And earnest prayers from a humble heart. But he'd learned not to expect much in return. Certainly not an answer.

At three o'clock one afternoon, he was caught up in a vision. Clear as day, he saw an angel of God, who strode forward and said, "Cornelius!"

Though a seasoned warrior, the centurion quaked from head to toe. "What do you want?"

"God has accepted your gifts, and he has heard your prayers."

Cornelius covered his face and whispered, "Thank you. All I have. Anything God asks. He can have it."

The angel spoke slowly and clearly, so that his message was

seared into the centurion's memory. "Send men to Joppa to bring back a man named Simon who is called Peter. He's staying with Simon the tanner, whose house is by the sea."

Then the heavenly messenger was gone. And Cornelius had his orders.

He acted upon them. And this righteous man who lived as an outsider received his welcome into God's family.

> While Peter was still speaking these words, the Holy Spirit came on all who heard the message. The circumcised believers who had come with Peter were astonished that the gift of the Holy Spirit had been poured out even on Gentiles.
>
> —Acts 10:44–45

Dig a Little Deeper

- According to Acts 10:28, what was the law where Gentiles were concerned? Can you imagine what this meant for Jewish Christians in the first century?
- How should we treat outsiders or those who are different from us?
- What is your heritage? Are there any interesting stories in your family tree? Who believed in God?

Q. When is an Angel not an Angel?

Q&A

> The one who is feeble among them in that day shall be like David, and the house of David *shall* be like God, like the Angel of the LORD before them.
>
> —ZECHARIAH 12:8 (NKJV)

There's a person in the Old Testament who's referred to as "the Angel of the Lord." The *A* in angel may be capitalized, depending on what translation of the Bible you're reading. So who is he? He's a recurring character. He's a prequel. He's the second person of the Trinity, or Godhead, *before* He was born into this world. In other words, He's Jesus ... or will be.

Hagar: In Gen. 16:6–14, the Angel of the Lord speaks with Hagar. How do we know this is the second person of the trinity? He's not the Father, since His name means *messenger of God.* And yet He accepts Hagar's reverence when she calls Him *El Roi,* meaning "the God who sees."

Manoah: Whenever humans try to bow down to angels, they are quick to say, "Don't worship me!" But the Angel of the Lord graciously accepts both worship and sacrifice. For example, Samson's parents meet Him, and they bring Him an offering, and He ascends to heaven in its flames (see Judg. 13). "When the angel of the LORD did not show himself again to Manoah and his wife, Manoah realized that it was the angel of the LORD" (Judg. 13:21).

Jacob: The Angel of God speaks to Jacob in Gen. 31:11–13, clearly stating, "I am the God of Bethel, where you anointed a pillar and where you made a vow to me."

So when is an Angel not an angel? When He's Jesus. The Angel of the Lord truly was "God with us," *Emmanuel*, in an earlier era. He's no angel. He's God!

Dig a Little Deeper

- Are you surprised to learn that Jesus was around before He was born? Why is this fact sort of mind-bending?

- According to Hebrews 1:2 and John 1:3, what did Jesus do long before He came to earth as the Son of God and the Son of Man?

- Father, Son, and Spirit work in perfect unison, yet in different ways. What's the Son's role (see John 3:16, 1 Tim. 2:5)?

THE TEMPTER CAME

Meeting an Angel

Then Jesus was led by the Spirit into the
wilderness to be tempted by the devil.

—MATTHEW 4:1

He always waited for weak moments. Finding his prey weak-ened by hunger, the devil greeted the Son of God with a smile. Oh, how weak the Almighty looked! In pitying tones, he feigned disbelief. "Is it you? Impossible. If you are who you claim to be, prove it! Tend to your needs. Tell these stones to become bread."

He heard the faint rumble of the man's stomach. Still, that didn't sway Jesus, who answered, "It is written: 'Man shall not live on bread alone, but on every word that comes from the mouth of God'" (Matt. 4:4).

Satan's jaw clenched, for words had always been *his* specialty. He didn't appreciate the reminder that this wasted, weary man had spoken every life into existence—including Satan's.

So the fallen one flaunted his power. Whisking Jesus away to the holy city, Satan lent Him his shoulder and helped Him to the pinnacle of the temple. From this high point, the tempter con-ceded, "Your words may have power. Shall we put them to the test? Because if you *are* the Son of God, a leap like this wouldn't be fatal." He lowered his voice. "You see, I know the Scriptures too. For it is written, 'He will command his angels concerning you, and they will lift you up in their hands, so that you will not strike your foot against a stone.'"

Oh, this was good! And on so many levels! A dare to flaunt it if you've got it. Biblical justification in the form of an unfulfilled prophecy. Even an oblique invitation to bring in reinforcements.

But Jesus wasn't impressed. "It is also written: 'Do not put the Lord your God to the test.'"

Barely concealing his rage, the devil swept Jesus to the highest of heights. One by one, he displayed the kingdoms of the world, along with their wealth and beauties. "Comfort and splendor. Wealth and dominion. I don't know what you expect to achieve with such humble beginnings, but if you'll bow down and worship me, this can be yours. I'll make a gift of it."

Divine authority sang through Jesus' next words. "Away from me, Satan! For it is written: 'Worship the Lord your God, and serve him only'" (Matt. 4:10).

And though it rankled him, the tempter had no choice but to go. For Jesus was indeed the Son of God, and His Word commanded the angels. Even fallen ones.

Dig a Little Deeper

- In what ways did Satan try to fluster or anger Jesus? Do these same things bug you?

- How did Jesus answer the tempter? What can you learn from Jesus' example?

- What does the Lord tell us about temptation in James 4:7?

MANNA

A Bible Lesson

This is the bread that came down from heaven.
Your ancestors ate manna and died, but
whoever feeds on this bread will live forever.

—JOHN 6:58

We don't know if angels actually need to eat, but the food God provided during the Israelites' wilderness wandering was known as angel's bread.

Human beings ate the bread of angels; he sent them all the food they could eat.

—PSALM 78:25

This miraculous stuff sustained God's people for years, the ultimate meal replacement. But when it first started showing up around their camp, the Israelites didn't know what to make of it.

That evening quail came and covered the camp, and in the morning there was a layer of dew around the camp. When the dew was gone, thin flakes like frost on the ground appeared on the desert floor. When the Israelites saw it, they said to each other, "What is it?" For they did not know what it was.

Moses said to them, "It is the bread the LORD has given you to eat."

—Exodus 16:13–15

Manna actually means, *what is it?* And folks did their best to describe it. They compared the color to white coriander, the taste to wafers and honey, and the look to flakes and sap (see Ex. 16:31, Num. 11:7).

Dig a Little Deeper

- What's your favorite flavor or food? Can you explain why?
- Would you like the chance to taste manna? What does Revelation 2:17 tell you about manna?
- In Psalm 34:8, what does David urge us to do? How can we do that?

DAY 26

Q. Does everyone have a guardian angel?

Q&A

He will cover you with his feathers, and
under his wings you will find refuge.
—Psalm 91:4

Most people I meet really, *really* want the answer to be *yes*. The truth is, we have no way of knowing for sure. You won't find the phrase *guardian angel* in the Bible, but there is one verse that hints at the possibility. Jesus said:

> See that you don't look down on one of these little ones. Here is what I tell you. Their angels in heaven are always with my Father who is in heaven."
> —Matthew 18:10 (NIrV)

I'll admit that it's an intriguing possibility. Wouldn't it be lovely if God's protection was given such a personal touch? Our very own angel. A hero to watch over us, to rescue us when danger creeps close, to shelter us under his wings. But I think the angelic hosts would be quick to point out that when they're sent to our side, it is proof of their sender's care.

> If you say, "The Lord is my refuge," and you make the Most High your dwelling, no harm will overtake you, no disaster will come near your tent. For he will command his angels concerning you to guard you in all

your ways; they will lift you up in their hands, so that you will not strike your foot against a stone.

—Psalm 91:9–12

Do you long for a rescuer? Are you searching for a pair of wings to crawl under? Would you welcome the dramatic entrance of a hero? Then ask God, because He's all that and more.

Dig a Little Deeper

- Who does David consider his guardian according to Psalm 25:20?
- How did Paul describe God's guardianship for him in 2 Timothy 4:18?
- According to Colossians 1:13, God comes to our rescue. From what? And where were we before?

MINISTERING SPIRITS
Meeting an Angel

Then the devil left him, and angels
came and attended him.
—MATTHEW 4:11

A way from me!" Jesus said, putting an end to the tempter's ploy. "For it is written: 'Worship the Lord your God, and serve Him only.'"

When Satan pitched Jesus back where He'd found Him, angels rushed to catch the Son of God, fulfilling the devil's previous taunt. "He will command his angels concerning you, and they will lift you up in their hands, so that you will not strike your foot against a stone" (Matt. 4:6).

"Fear not," they said, gathering Him up.

"We are sent to serve."

"Let us attend you."

Resisting the devil had been one thing. Resisting his angels was unnecessary. Jesus' fast was over. His ministry could begin. But not until His own ministered to Him. After forty days and forty nights without food, the Son of God's very human body was worn down.

The angels offered Him better food than stone turned into bread. They gave Him manna to eat, the bread of angels. Washing and water. Kind words and smiles. Songs and sleep. He needed their ministry, and thanked the Father who'd sent them.

With reverence and affection, they cared for Jesus, glad to fulfill their part in God's plan. Then He returned to Galilee in full power, teaching and glorifying God.

Dig a Little Deeper

- After spending forty days with His enemy in the wilderness, what do you think Jesus needed most?

- Why would angels have a different perspective on Bible stories than the humans involved?

- Why are they different from ours?

Q. Do Angels Sing?

Q&A

And I saw a mighty angel
proclaiming in a loud voice ...
—REVELATION 5:2

Whenever Christmas comes around, we hear about the choirs of angels that filled the Bethlehem sky, singing in celebration of the newborn Son of God. "Sing, choirs of angels, sing in exultation; sing all ye citizens of heaven above!"

However, theologians are fond of pointing out that angels never sing in the Bible. Not once. They speak, shout, declare, praise, and proclaim, but there's no biblical record of a melody line. Does that mean angels don't sing? Not necessarily.

So what *does* an angel sound like?

A Call: There were times when people heard a voice in the sky, like when Hagar encountered an angel in the desert. "The angel of God called to Hagar from heaven and said to her, 'What is the matter, Hagar? Do not be afraid ...'" (Gen. 21:17).

A Loud Voice: In John's Revelation, he describes the arrival of an angel with a good set of lungs. "And I saw a mighty angel proclaiming in a loud voice, 'Who is worthy to break the seals and open the scroll?'" (Rev. 5:2).

A Roar: As the book of Revelation continues, the noise levels escalate, and it's time to shout! "Then I saw another mighty angel coming down from heaven ... and he gave a loud shout like the roar of a lion" (Rev. 10:1, 3).

Thunder: When the people crowded along the Jordan River to see John baptize Jesus, they heard God speak. But not everyone understood what they'd heard. Some heard it and said it was thunder; others said an angel must have spoken (see John 12:29), which falls in line with what John later wrote in Revelation 10:3–4. "When he [the angel] shouted, the voices of the seven thunders spoke."

Paul also saw an angel during a vision on his voyage to Rome (see Acts 27:21–24), so he knew firsthand if the voice of an angel was loud, fierce, lovely, or lyrical.

Maybe there are songs. Maybe angels' shouts ring from one end of heaven to the next. Maybe they speak of things that are and were and will forever be. One day we'll get to tune in.

Dig a Little Deeper

- How is singing together different from listening to a performance?
- Why do you suppose music is able to bridge language gaps? How can God use this for His kingdom?
- Will there be songs in heaven (see Rev. 5:9 and 15:3)?

AMONG THE MYRTLE TREES

Meeting an Angel

So the LORD replied with kind and
comforting words. He spoke them to
the angel who talked with me.

—ZECHARIAH 1:13 (NIRV)

Zechariah saw the Angel of the Lord in a vision. While he was watching, the commander of heaven's hosts came riding upon a red horse. Zechariah caught up to him in a ravine, where the commander stood among the myrtle trees. There were more horses with him—red, brown, and white—so Zechariah asked about them. "What are these?"

One of his angels explained that the Lord had sent these horses throughout the whole earth. And in returning to the myrtle grove, they brought a report.

"What did you find?" asked the Angel of the Lord.

And they answered, "The whole world is at rest and in peace."

The Lord spoke kindly to the angel who talked with Zechariah. His words were a comfort, but also a command. He told Zechariah to speak the words of God. And he poured out words of love and mercy for Jerusalem and Zion. The Lord Almighty gave me a message of peace. "My towns will again overflow with prosperity, and the LORD will again comfort Zion and choose Jerusalem" (Zech. 1:17).

And after many similar visions, the word of the Lord came to Zechariah with a prophecy and a promise. Zion's King would come:

> Rejoice greatly, O daughter of Zion! Shout, O daughter of Jerusalem! Behold, your King *is* coming to you; He is just and having salvation, Lowly and riding on a donkey, a colt, the foal of a donkey ... He shall speak peace to the nations; His dominion *shall* be "from sea to sea, and from the River to the ends of the earth."
> —ZECHARIAH 9:9–10 (NJKV)

Dig a Little Deeper

- How did Zechariah's experience with angelic visitors differ from the usual bout of fear and trembling?

- Have you ever dreamed about heavenly things? What's the difference between a dream and a vision?

- Which parts of Zechariah's prophecy were fulfilled in Matthew 21:1–10? What remains to occur?

Q. Do angels sit around on clouds all day, playing harps?

Q&A

Praise the LORD, you his angels, you mighty ones
who do his bidding, who obey his word.

—PSALM 103:20

Angels are God's servants. They live to do His bidding. In Hebrews 1:14, angels are described as "ministering spirits sent to serve those who will inherit salvation." Which means they're probably not lazing around plucking at harp strings. God's servants have roles to fulfill.

Angels are often found in praise. These worshipers live to exalt their creator.

> And they were calling to one another: "Holy, holy, holy is the LORD Almighty; the whole earth is full of his glory."
>
> —ISAIAH 6:3

Angels also act as God's messengers, bringing news either firsthand or in dreams.

> In the visions I saw while lying in bed, I looked, and there before me was a holy one, a messenger, coming down from heaven.
>
> —DANIEL 4:13

Angels are mighty warriors, protectors who are ready to defend heaven against its enemies.

> Then war broke out in heaven. Michael and his angels fought against the dragon, and the dragon and his angels fought back.
>
> —REVELATION 12:7

Angels can act as caretakers, ministering to those in need of comfort or care.

> An angel from heaven appeared to him and strengthened him.
>
> —LUKE 22:43

Angels will act as guardians, stepping in to prevent people from coming to harm.

> For he will command his angels concerning you to guard you in all your ways; they will lift you up in their hands, so that you will not strike your foot against a stone.
>
> —PSALM 91:11–12

Angels are keen observers of God's redemptive plan, watching His hand at work in the world.

> There is rejoicing in the presence of the angels of God over one sinner who repents.
>
> —LUKE 15:10

Dig a Little Deeper

- Like angels, people have different gifts, talents, and roles within God's family. Read Romans 12:6–8. Can you see yourself in Paul's list? What gifts and talents would you add?
- How would you describe your personality? What makes you uniquely you?
- What are your gifts, talents, and roles for serving God?

I Must Be Dreaming

Meeting an Angel

> Suddenly an angel of the Lord appeared
> and a light shone in the cell.
> —Acts 12:7

Peter rolled his aching shoulders as the night air seeped into his bones. Shackles prevented him from reaching his clothes, which the guards had tossed into the opposite corner. Wrists raw. Back bruised. Head aching. It wasn't much worse than a rough day at the oars. The discomfort was hardly worth mentioning, given how much His Lord had suffered.

Fears and frustration roiled in Peter's gut. He remembered what it was like, watching soldiers drag away his leader. Once more, the people who believed in Christ were sheep without a shepherd. And there was nothing he could do to comfort them. Except pray.

Through the long watches of the night, Peter poured out his heart. For his friends and family. For the church's safety, for their courage, their peace. All for the sake of the gospel. All for the glory of God.

A sharp jab to the ribs roused him from a fitful doze. Had the guard kicked him? Peter squinted against the sudden light. Was it morning? But a man in shining clothes knelt beside him, brighter than any dawn.

"Quick!" the angel urged, beckoning for him to rise.

Peter mutely showed him the heavy shackles that kept him prisoner.

With a touch, the chains fell away. "Get up."

Struggling to coordinate numb limbs, Peter rose stiffly and hugged himself. Was this a dream?

The angel picked up the crumpled garments and brought them over. "Put on your clothes."

Again, Peter obeyed ... with a little help from his shining guest.

"Sandals." And once those were in place, the angel said, "Wrap your cloak around you and follow me."

Peter's heart beat faster at the familiar call to follow. Wasn't that how everything had begun?

He plodded after the angel, thinking that this was a very strange dream. Guards stood as though blind. Locked doors swung wide. Even when the prison gate opened, no one raised an alarm. A quiet street. A glimpse of the stars. A question on his lips. But before his questions could lead to answers, Peter had his.

The Lord had sent His angel. And in obeying the call to follow, Peter had found freedom.

Dig a Little Deeper

- Read Acts 12:12. Whose prayers were answered when the angel arrived to set Peter free?

- Have you ever been in a situation where the only thing you could do was pray?

- How often do you pray for yourself? How often do you pray for others?

Q. How are angels different from God?

Q&A

> God is highly respected among his
> holy angels. He's more wonderful than
> all those who are around him.
> —Psalm 89:7 (NIrV)

Only God is God. No one else can match His perfection. Not even the angels. As the psalmist says, "Who in the skies above can compare with the Lord? Who among the angels is like the Lord?" (Ps. 89:6 NIrV). But I'm sometimes asked how angels are different from God. And also how humans compare to angels. Here's a fun place to begin that conversation:

No beginning, no end: God is completely unique in that He has no beginning and no end. He's been around since forever, and He'll go on forever. "I am the Alpha and the Omega,' says the Lord God, 'who is, and who was, and who is to come, the Almighty" (Rev. 1:8).

A beginning, no end: God created everything. Angels are created beings, so they have a beginning, but their lives have no end. When sin entered the world, death derailed the eternal paradise God intended for humanity. As a consequence of humanity's fall, life would end in death. That was the cost of sin (see Rom. 6:23). In much the same way, the fallen angels know that their end is sure (see Matt. 25:41; Rev. 20:14). Angels will live with God forever, though, in heaven (see Luke 20:36).

A beginning, no end: "The gift of God is eternal life" (Rom. 6:23), which means believers are changed. We are "like the angels" (Luke 20:36) because we can no longer die. So Christians are like God's faithful servants in heaven, having a beginning but no end.

God is unique in that He has no beginning and no end. Angels are created beings, so they have a beginning, but their lives have no end. Fallen angels and fallen humans face an end. That's the consequence of sin, and that's why we need a Savior. Christians become the "children of the resurrection" (Luke 20:36) and will join the angels in heaven for eternity.

Dig a Little Deeper

- Angels may fascinate us forever, but the Bible says that God is even more amazing. What are some of the other amazing works of God?

- What similarities do you have with an angel?

- How can God's knowledge and power be in your life?

GOD SEES ME

Meeting an Angel

Then the angel of the LORD told her, "Go back to your mistress and submit to her." The angel added, "I will increase your descendants so much that they will be too numerous to count."

—GENESIS 16:9–10

A hundred slights. A thousand unkind words. All of Sarai's confident plans had twisted into persecution. *It was her plan,* Hagar thought. *She gave me to her husband, and he was kind to me.*

Yet Abram turned a blind eye to his wife's cruelty, leaving Hagar with nothing but ash and bitterness. And morning sickness. Had it been so wrong to hope for her master's attention? Did she not deserve to be elevated, now that she carried Abram's heir? Yet she had become worse than a dog, to be kicked and cursed at every turn.

Shuffling into the sparse shade of a squat tree, Hagar sipped what was left of her water. In this desert, she needed shelter. Hot by day. Cold by night. And lonely. Without help, she wouldn't be able to move the spring's stone. And who knew what kind of men might come along. Dashing away angry tears, Hagar tried to convince herself that it didn't matter. She was a slave, and her master's child would die with her.

"Hagar, servant of Sarai, where have you come from, and where are you going?"

The woman flinched away from the man who knew her name. No, *not* a man. Perhaps death was closer than she'd thought. Why else would she be seeing an angel? Clutching the empty water skin to her chest, she told the truth. "I'm running away from my mistress."

He shook his head and commanded, "Go back to Sarai and serve her."

"Do you know what you're asking?"

The angel answered, "You will have a son. And God is going to increase your descendants so that they are too numerous to count."

Hagar's heartbeat quickened. Abram may have turned away from her, but God had seen her distress. The promise the Lord had made to her master would be fulfilled through her son.

"You shall name him Ishmael, for the Lord has heard of your misery."

It was true! She wasn't alone. God would be faithful to her and to His promise. Bowing her head, Hagar gave the Lord a name. "I have seen the One who sees me, so you are the God who sees me."

Dig a Little Deeper

- Have you ever trusted someone, only to have everything go very wrong?

- How do you deal with unhappiness? Where do you go for comfort?

- What promises does God give to His children (see Ps. 68:19, Isa. 41:10, Matt. 6:25–32, John 14:16)?

Q. CAN I TALK TO MY ANGEL?

Q&A

Some people ... worship angels. But don't let people like that judge you ... Their minds are not guided by the Holy Spirit.

—COLOSSIANS 2:18 (NIrV)

First, we don't know for sure that there is a guardian angel watching over each of us. That said, it's important to remember that any angel guarding us doesn't truly belong to us. He's God's. All the angels are. If a guardian angel is nearby, he's not there for a chat. I'll admit that it's nice to imagine forming a bond with an angelic bestie. But don't let wishful thinking get between you and the God who sends His servants to your aid. The relationship we need to nurture is with the Father.

Don't look for angels: God's ways are mysterious. Who can say why He does what He does. Those who met angels weren't on the lookout for a close encounter of the heavenly kind. There's not much point in taking up angel-spotting as a hobby. Instead, find ways to *be* an angel for others, and maybe in the process, you'll entertain a real one without knowing it (see Heb. 13:2).

Don't pray to angels: Striking up a conversation with the supernatural is essentially prayer. And praying to anyone other than God is idolatry. Did you know that many of the false gods worshiped in ancient times were actually fallen angels (see Deut. 32:17 NKJV)? The Bible also sternly warns against conversing with "familiar spirits" (Lev. 20:6 NKJV).

Don't worship angels: Angel worship has been around for centuries. Paul warns believers against it (see Col. 2:18), but what's really wonderful is that the Bible gives us an angel's perspective on this issue.

> At this I fell at his feet to worship him. But he said to me, "Don't do that! I am a fellow servant with you and with your brothers and sisters who hold to the testimony of Jesus. Worship God! For it is the Spirit of prophecy who bears testimony to Jesus."
>
> —REVELATION 19:10

> But he said to me, "Don't do that! I am a fellow servant with you and with your fellow prophets and with all who keep the words of this scroll. Worship God!"
>
> —REVELATION 22:9

Angels don't want to steal any of the glory that belongs to God. They are quick to correct those who mistakenly bow to them. God's faithful angels will never welcome our praise.

Dig a Little Deeper

- How would you explain prayer to someone unfamiliar with God?
- How does thinking of angels as fellow servants change how you think of them? How does it shape how you think of the God who created them?
- In what way can you support your other fellow servants? How can you encourage fellow believers?

LEGION

Meeting an Angel

> For Jesus had commanded the impure spirit to
> come out of the man ... And they begged Jesus
> repeatedly not to order them to go into the Abyss.
>
> —LUKE 8:29, 31

Peter expertly guided the boat to shore. The moment the hull *shuffed* into the soft sand in the shallows, his brother Andrew was over the side, hauling them aground before scanning the vicinity. "This is a Gentile city," he remarked.

Joining him, Peter eyed the tombs dotting the hillside above the lakeside village. "I don't like it."

But Jesus strode past them. Focused. Purposeful.

Trading a glance, the disciples hurried after him.

"Look there!" exclaimed Andrew, pointing.

Suddenly, a naked man shambled forward from the nearby graveyard. Filth marred his skin. Spittle clung to his grizzled beard. Dried blood caked on his festering wounds and drew flies. As the man neared the beach, Jesus stood His ground.

The man flung his arms wide and yelled, "What do you want with me, Jesus, Son of the Most High God?"

"What did he say?" asked John.

James shook his head. "He's mad. He can't know what he's saying."

"We've seen this before." Peter shouldered an oar and kept a wary eye on the wild man. "There's a demon at work."

Jesus raised His voice. "Come out of this man, you evil spirit."

Peter's skin crawled when a ragged voice argued, "Swear to God that you won't torture me!"

Striding closer, the Lord asked, "What's your name?"

The possessed man cowered and turned, pulling at his hair and scraping ragged nails across old wounds. But he obediently answered. "My name is Legion, for we are many."

When Jesus reached toward him, the man cried out. The Lord gazed straight into the trembling captive's face, but the man avoided Jesus' gaze, eyes rolling to the side. That's when the captor spied a way of escape.

In shrill tones, Legion begged, "Send us among the pigs! Allow us to go into them!"

Jesus answered, "Be gone."

A moment later, the herd of pigs panicked. Squealing and chomping, the animals scattered, causing such a commotion that Jesus' followers crowded together. While everyone else's attention was fixed on the converging stampede, Peter's eyes never left the man, who'd sagged into his Savior's embrace.

"My lord?" the man croaked.

Removing His cloak, Jesus gently wrapped it around the freed man's shoulders. "I am He."

The man clung even more tightly, and his words were so broken by sobs that Peter couldn't catch their meaning. Tugging his brother's sleeve he asked, "What's he saying?"

Andrew answered, *"Thank you."*

Dig a Little Deeper

- Something similar happened in Luke 4:33–34. Demons recognized Jesus. Even though they're the enemy, how does this help confirm the faith of His followers?

- According to Luke 4:18, what prophecy did Jesus come to fulfill?

- When Jesus rescues people out of great darkness, what kind of life does He lead them into (see 1 Pet. 2:9)?

Q. ARE DEMONS ANGELS?

Q&A

> For since the message spoken through angels was binding, and every violation and disobedience received its just punishment, how shall we escape if we ignore so great a salvation?
>
> —HEBREWS 2:2–3

Demons are angels who used to belong to heaven. They were servants of God, but they were cast out for disobedience. In short, they sinned. Like Adam and Eve, who were driven out of Eden when mankind fell, angels who disobeyed were cast to earth.

> God did not spare angels when they sinned, but sent them to hell, putting them in chains of darkness to be held for judgment.
>
> —2 PETER 2:4

> And the angels who did not keep their positions of authority but abandoned their proper dwelling—these he has kept in darkness, bound with everlasting chains for judgment on the great Day.
>
> —JUDE 1:6

They became enemies of God, which is a little different than how it works for humans. Because of the sin of Adam and Eve, we're born enemies of God (see Rom. 5:10). Sin is part of our DNA, but Jesus' sacrifice can reverse the effects of the fall. Believers become servants of God, and we belong to heaven.

Sin sealed the devil's fate and that of the angels who followed him, for its price has always been death (see Rom. 6:23).

Dig a Little Deeper

- How was the fall of angels similar to the fall of humanity? What were the consequences?
- Why are the choices we make every day important?
- What can we do about our sin (see 1 John 1:9)?

SURROUNDING THE LION

A Bible Lesson

Your adversary the devil walks about like
a roaring lion, seeking whom he may
devour. Resist him, steadfast in the faith.

—1 PETER 5:8–9 (NKJV)

Have you ever been minding your own business, strolling along without a care in the world, when suddenly a critter skitters across your path? Mouse. Lizard. Or my personal least-favorite—spider! And *wham*! You jump three feet, make undignified noises, and start looking for high ground.

"That thing had to be eight inches! Maybe ten!" By the time we're telling our harrowing tale to friends, the spider is a foot wide and bared its mandibles before retreating into the shrubbery. It's as if fear upgrades our eyes with zoom lenses, and our enemy of the moment is bigger than life.

I think that's what happens to a lot of us when we think about fallen angels or read Peter's description of Satan in 1 Peter 5:8. As soon as we see the "lion," he's all we can see. But before you curl up in some corner for fear of unseen monsters, look at the whole paragraph. Peter is speaking to young people, and he offers both advice and promises.

Be humble: The first thing Peter calls for is an attitude check. "Submit yourselves to *your* elders" (5:5). Pride led to the devil's own downfall. Beware, or it'll sneak in—me first, my way, me, me, *me*! Peter reminds us that "God opposes the proud but gives grace to the humble." What does humility look like in this passage? Obey your parents. Be nice to others. Wait your turn.

Don't worry: Next, Peter urges us not to worry about stuff. God's got this. We're under His mighty hand (see 5:6). The following verse is worth memorizing: "Cast all your anxiety on him because he cares for you" (5:7). God knows you have cares and concerns, and He wants to take them off your hands. Why? Because you matter to Him. He'll take care of you.

Resist temptation: Now the devil prowls onto the scene. Peter warns, "Be alert and of sober mind" (5:8). There's danger, but it's one we can resist. How? By standing firm. By saying *no*. By doing the right thing.

You're not alone: It's not always easy. Which is another way of saying, "It's *hard*!" And when we're in the middle of a mess, the mess is all we can see. So we get discouraged and wonder, "Why me?" But Peter says, "The family of believers throughout the world is undergoing the same kind of sufferings" (5:9). Such is life. Hang in there.

God called you: Life can leave us feeling small, weak, and unnoticed. Throw in a rampaging spider, a mistake or two, and loneliness, and it's more than we can handle. That's why Peter shakes up our perspective with verse 10. God picked you, and He'll hold your hand through any mess. Feeling unequal to the task? That's okay. He'll "restore you and make you strong, firm and steadfast" (5:10). By His power, you can make it a little while longer.

To him be the power for ever and ever. Amen.

—1 PETER 5:11

Dig a Little Deeper

- Which words in 1 Peter 5:5–11 do you find hardest to believe or live by?
- Who is always stronger than Satan or any fallen angel?
- How does your fear change once you believe God is on your side?

Q. Are there female angels?

Q&A

> They will be like the angels in heaven.
> —Mark 12:25

There's a lot of angel art out there. Delicate porcelain figurines. Ethereal portraits. Classic illustrations. Christmas tree toppers. And in nearly every instance, these angels are portrayed as beautiful women. Is it any wonder there's confusion over this point? Angels are spiritual beings; they are not male or female. Here's what we know about angels from the Bible.

Angels weren't created to marry: In Matthew 22:30 and Mark 12:25, Jesus said there is no marriage for humans in heaven since we will be like the angels. So marriage wasn't part of God's design for angels.

Angels take on the human form of men: Abraham, Hagar, Jacob, Lot, Daniel, Mary, Philip, John—in each instance where people met angels, their heavenly visitors are described as men.

Angels may have mixed with humans: In Genesis 6:2, we're told, "The sons of God saw that the daughters of humans were beautiful, and they married any of them they chose." Some have interpreted this as an intermingling of angels with humanity. "The Nephilim were on the earth in those days—and also afterward—when the sons of God went to the daughters of humans and had children by them. They were the heroes of old, men of renown" (Gen. 6:4). Since this is the only verse of its kind in the Bible, there isn't enough information to answer more questions, but it's another hint that angels took male form.

Dig a Little Deeper

- Do you have any angel art around the house? How does it present angels?
- What has shaped your idea of what an angel should be?
- If someone was described as "angelic," what does that usually mean? How does that compare with the description of angels in the Bible?

HEAVENLY VISITOR
Meeting an Angel

A man of God came to me. He looked
like an angel of God, very awesome.

—JUDGES 13:6

Manoah wasn't sure what to make of his wife's story. Perhaps it was wishful thinking, or she'd been taken by a daydream. Even after many years as husband and wife, they'd been unable to have a child. Could her wish for a baby have made her crazy? But he'd questioned her closely, and she had insisted that a wonderful man had spoken to her like a prophet.

Manoah tugged at his beard and wondered if he should bring his wife to a priest. Perhaps they could confirm her story. Manoah had been praying for confirmation.

"Husband! Husband!" came his wife's voice. "Your prayers are answered! He's back!"

Hurrying outside, Manoah followed his wife into their fields. Just as she'd said, the man was truly impressive, as bright and beautiful as an angel from on high.

Manoah stepped forward and demanded, "What about these rules? Will our son truly be able to deliver us from the Philistines?"

"She must follow every instruction without exception."

Manoah glanced at his wife, whose smug expression said,

I told you so. But he wouldn't begrudge her this triumph. The prophet's news was welcome. Recalling his manners, Manoah asked the man to stay for dinner.

"Even if you insist, I won't eat your food. But if you prepare a burnt offering, sacrifice it to the Lord."

"We will!" Manoah quickly agreed. "Only … what is your name?"

"Why do you ask?" the man replied. "It is beyond understanding."

That was a strange answer. But, still, Manoah prepared both a goat and a grain offering, sacrificing both to the Lord upon a rock. And while he and his wife watched, flames blazed up from the altar toward heaven. And even more staggering, the man ascended with them.

The woman gave birth to a boy and named him Samson.

—JUDGES 13:24

Dig a Little Deeper

- How do you usually react to news that's too good to be true?
- When God answered the prayers of Manoah and his wife, it wasn't just for them. What would their son do for God's people?
- How can God answer your prayers in a way that reaches others? Will that change how you pray?

HOSPITALITY TO ANGELS
A Bible Lesson

Do not forget to show hospitality to strangers,
for by so doing some people have shown
hospitality to angels without knowing it.

—HEBREWS 13:2

Abraham was relaxing in his tent's entrance when he noticed three men standing in the shade of the terebinth trees. With a soft huff, he levered to his feet. Where had his mind been wandering? His favorite seat had an excellent view of the road, so he didn't usually miss the approach of travelers.

Bowing low to the men, he said, "Welcome, my lords. Look favorably on your servant and do not pass us by. I'll bring some water. Rest in this shade, and I'll bring refreshments."

In back-to-back chapters of Genesis (18–19), both Abraham and Lot offered hospitality to strangers, unaware that the men they invited into their homes were supernatural beings.

Abraham pulled out all the stops and provided a feast for his three guests, who brought welcome news. He and his wife, Sarah, would have a son in his old age, and the boy's name would mean "laughter." But their after-dinner conversation turned to serious matters.

Two of the great cities on the plain were slated for destruction. And in pleading with the Lord and His angels on behalf of any righteous men remaining in Sodom and Gomorrah, Abraham saved his nephew Lot's life.

> The two angels arrived at Sodom in the evening, and Lot was sitting in the gateway of the city. When he saw them, he got up to meet them and bowed down with his face to the ground. "My lords," he said, "please turn aside to your servant's house. You can wash your feet and spend the night and then go on your way early in the morning."
>
> —GENESIS 19:1–2

Just like his uncle, Lot showed hospitality to the strangers. He didn't have a clue that they were angels, yet he went to great lengths to protect them from the dangers of his city. But Lot's heavenly guests rushed him and his family out of the city. They dragged their feet the whole way, but God found a way to rescue them. Abraham's plea became Lot's miracle (see Gen. 19:27–29).

Abraham's generosity. Lot's hospitality. They were small things. You could say that anyone in that time and place would have been as kind. But in these miraculous meetings, God listened to their pleas. Tragedy was averted. Lives were saved. And God showed mercy.

Dig a Little Deeper

- What are the similarities between Abraham's welcome (see Gen. 18:1–5) and Lot's welcome (see Gen. 19:1–2)? Yet these encounters ended so differently. Can you pinpoint some key differences between these two hosts?

- What do you think of when you hear the word *hospitality*? Probably not a glass of water and foot-scrubbing followed by grilled goat. So how do you treat guests in your corner of the world?

- How does generosity affect the person receiving it? What about the giver?

Q. WHERE IS PETER'S GATE?

Q&A

You are Peter. On this rock I will build my church. The gates of hell will not be strong enough to destroy it. I will give you the keys to the kingdom of heaven.

—MATTHEW 16:18–19 (NIrV)

In pop culture, Peter is often portrayed as heaven's gatekeeper. The only way to enter paradise is for him to find your name on his list. Or people must correctly answer his questions in order for him to open the gate.

Oddly enough, the rumor started with Jesus. While in Caesarea Philippi, Jesus gave Simon a new name while talking about God's kingdom. "You are Peter, and on this rock I will build my church, and the gates of Hades will not overcome it. I will give you the keys of the kingdom of heaven" (Matt. 16:18–19). Jesus wasn't handing over an actual set of keys, and He certainly wasn't describing Peter's new post as heaven's checkpoint guard. There was an object lesson underway in which Jesus opened the gates of His kingdom to all believers.

Naturally, Peter's Gate is a myth, but there *will* be gates. And the gatekeepers of the heavenly city are angels. Twelve of them.

It had a great, high wall with twelve gates, and with twelve angels at the gates. On the gates were written the names of the twelve tribes of Israel.

—REVELATION 21:12

Peter's Gate may be a myth, but the pearly gates are the truth. So are the streets of gold. We find their description later in the same chapter of Revelation.

> The twelve gates were twelve pearls, each gate made of a single pearl. The great street of the city was of gold, as pure as transparent glass.
>
> —REVELATION 21:21

One day we will see these beauties because Jesus made a way for Peter, His disciples, and all His followers.

Dig a Little Deeper

- In Matthew 7:13–14, what does Jesus say about the way into heaven?
- How did you first hear about Jesus?
- What does Paul say has always been God's plan, according to Acts 17:26–27?

SEE ME OFF

Meeting an Angel

As they were walking along and talking together,
suddenly a chariot of fire and horses of fire
appeared and separated the two of them, and
Elijah went up to heaven in a whirlwind.

—2 KINGS 2:11

Stay here. I'm going to Bethel."

"I'm coming along." Elisha usually did as he was told, but nothing would stop him from keeping his usual place at Elijah's side. Not on this day. With a stubborn lift of his chin, Elisha promised, "As surely as the Lord lives and you live, I will not leave you."

Although the journey was uneventful, a crowd waited on the outskirts of Bethel.

"I'll see what they want," Elisha said.

The milling group turned out to be prophets, and their message was for him. "The Lord will take your master from you today," announced their spokesman. "Did you know?"

"I know," Elisha grumbled, glancing back to where Elijah rested in the shade. "I know it, and I don't want to talk about it."

"Elisha!"

"I am here," he replied, hurrying back to his master's side. "What do you need?"

"This is far enough. Stay put." Gesturing toward the wilderness to the east, he said, "God is sending me to Jericho."

Swallowing hard, Elisha repeated his oath. "As surely as the Lord lives and you live, I will not leave you."

So they took the road to Jericho.

Once again, they came upon another group of prophets. Elisha had a good idea what they wanted.

"Elisha," called their leader. "Do you know that the Lord is going to take your master from you today?"

"I know, I know," he sighed. "Just leave it."

Of course, Elijah had also received a word from the Lord. "Why don't you stay here? I'm going to the Jordan next."

Although his voice cracked with emotion, Elisha renewed his vow. "As surely as the Lord lives and you live, I will not leave you."

So the two of them walked on. It wasn't far to the river. Fifty of the prophets followed, although they kept a polite distance, remaining on the opposite bank while Elijah parted the water and led Elisha across.

"You know what is coming?" Elijah asked.

Elisha's voice shook. "I don't want to say good-bye."

"You've been like my own son," Elijah said. "Tell me. What can I do for you before I am taken away?"

If his master couldn't stay, perhaps God would give him the strength to go on alone. Elisha replied, "Let me inherit a double portion of your spirit."

Elijah pulled him close and handed down heaven's answer. "You are asking for something difficult, but if you see me off, God will grant it."

"I will not leave you!" Elisha repeated.

"And yet I must leave you," Elijah murmured.

They walked along slowly, prolonging their last minutes. But the wind suddenly changed, and they turned together. Elisha trembled, for a chariot of fire drawn by flaming horses bore down on them. He stood frozen by dread, fear, and fascination, but Elijah pushed him out of its path. Separated by the heavenly conveyance, Elisha scrambled to his feet and searched for his master. He started running and shouted, but Elijah's gaze was fixed on something that put a shine on his face. The time had come. God's angels were here to take him up.

"Elijah! *Father!*" Heart pounding, Elisha squinted against the winds that whipped up. Though his heart was breaking, he would not look away. Even though it was difficult, this is what God had asked of Elisha. He would see his father off.

Dig a Little Deeper

- In Matthew 17:10–12, what did Jesus confirm about Elijah? What role was he to fulfill? (Compare to Jesus' statement in Matthew 11:10–14.)

- What promise was given to Zechariah about his son, John, in Luke 1:17?

- Who has a New Testament cameo in Luke 9:30–33?

MICHAEL

A Bible Lesson

> Then Michael, one of the chief princes, came
> to help me, because I was detained.
>
> —DANIEL 10:13

Only two of God's angels are mentioned by name in the Bible. The first is Gabriel. The second is Michael, who is called an archangel. Let's take a look at the three passages in which he's mentioned. The first is in Daniel, when a shining man appears before Daniel. This angel was a messenger who was delayed by an enemy, and he was only able to complete his assignment because Michael came to his rescue.

> He said, "Daniel, you who are highly esteemed, consider carefully the words I am about to speak to you, and stand up, for I have now been sent to you." And when he said this to me, I stood up trembling.
>
> Then he continued, "Do not be afraid, Daniel. Since the first day that you set your mind to gain understanding and to humble yourself before your God, your words were heard, and I have come in response to them. But the prince of the Persian kingdom resisted me twenty-one days. Then Michael, one of the chief princes, came to help me, because I was detained there with the king of Persia."
>
> —DANIEL 10:11–13

In the New Testament book of Jude, this brother of Jesus warns Christians about godless people who twist the Scriptures to suit themselves. Jude compares these sinners to fallen angels, who "pollute their own bodies, reject authority and heap abuse on celestial beings" (Jude 1:8). By contrast, he holds up the example set by Michael.

> But even the archangel Michael, when he was disputing with the devil about the body of Moses, did not himself dare to condemn him for slander but said, "The Lord rebuke you!"
>
> —JUDE 1:9

And finally, Michael is mentioned in the book of Revelation. In this exciting passage, Michael is clearly shown as a leader, for he leads angels in an epic battle against Satan, who took the form of a dragon.

> Then war broke out in heaven. Michael and his angels fought against the dragon, and the dragon and his angels fought back. But he was not strong enough, and they lost their place in heaven. The great dragon was hurled down—that ancient serpent called the devil, or Satan, who leads the whole world astray. He was hurled to the earth, and his angels with him.
>
> —REVELATION 12:7–9

Dig a Little Deeper

- What ideas does the term *prince* conjure up in your mind when you think about angels?
- Is it strange to think that there are real battles happening all around us? What does the Bible tell us about spiritual warfare (see 2 Cor. 10:3–4, Eph. 6:10–13, 2 Tim. 4:18)?
- What part do our prayers play in God's plans (see Eph. 6:18)?

Q. WHAT DO ANGELS AND THUNDERSTORMS HAVE IN COMMON?

Q&A

His appearance was like lightning, and
his clothes were white as snow.

—MATTHEW 28:3

There's an old story that people tell children who are frightened when the sky rumbles. They'll say, "Don't be afraid. It's just the angels bowling." Does thunder sound like the roll and crash of pins when someone bowls a strike? Maybe a little, but angels aren't the force behind thunderclaps. The similarity between them and these storms lies in lightning. Consider these verses about the appearance of heaven's messengers:

The appearance of the living creatures was like burning coals of fire or like torches. Fire moved back and forth among the creatures; it was bright, and lightning flashed out of it. The creatures sped back and forth like flashes of lightning.

—EZEKIEL 1:13–14

An angel of the Lord appeared to them, and the glory of the Lord shone around them, and they were terrified.

—LUKE 2:9

> While they were wondering about this, suddenly two men in clothes that gleamed like lightning stood beside them.
>
> —LUKE 24:4

If you've ever had to squint because a sudden flash of lightning dazzled your eyes, you know how sudden and brilliant an angel's appearance can be!

Dig a Little Deeper

- Do you like thunderstorms? Why or why not?
- What is often associated with the presence of God (see Ex. 19:16, Job 26:14, Isa. 29:6, Rev. 4:5)?
- By contrast, look at how God spoke to Elijah in 1 Kings 19:11–12. What else does that tell you about God?

THE LORD IS PEACE

Meeting an Angel

The angel of the LORD came and sat down under the oak in Ophrah that belonged to Joash the Abiezrite, where his son Gideon was threshing wheat.

—JUDGES 6:11

Gideon's back was breaking. Threshing without a whisper of wind was difficult. But, a cloud of chaff shimmering in the sun would draw unwanted attention from camel-riding marauders.

"They're a plague of locusts on our land," Gideon said to himself through gritted teeth. The Midianites were unwanted guests in Israel—oppressors who forced God's people to crowd into strongholds, mountain clefts, and caves.

"Their herds graze on our fields; their tents darken our hill-tops. They have ravaged us until we're too weak to fight back." If Gideon couldn't keep this part of their harvest hidden, his brothers and sisters would starve.

With a grim shake of his head, Gideon asked, "How much longer can we live like this?"

A voice answered from the direction of the oak tree whose branches sheltered the winepress. "The Lord is with you, mighty warrior."

Gideon held up his rake in defense. He eyed the stranger warily. Satisfied the newcomer wasn't a Midianite scout, he retorted,

"If the Lord is truly with us, why has all this happened?" Turning his back, Gideon concluded, "God has abandoned us."

"I am here, and I will send you. Go and save Israel."

"Me?" Shouldering the rake, Gideon stared at the stranger in frank disbelief. "My clan is the weakest in Manasseh, and I am the least in my family. Someone like me can't save our nation."

"I will be with you," the stranger promised. "You will rid the land of them once and for all."

It was too good to be true. Adopting a cautious tone, Gideon said, "If I've truly found favor in your eyes, give me a sign that it's really you. If you want, I'll bring an offering to set before you."

Though food was scarce, Gideon did his best, preparing tender meat in broth and flat bread. Putting the meal in a basket, he brought it back to the shelter of the oak tree and placed them on a stone. He poured out the broth as he'd been instructed.

With the tip of his staff, the stranger touched the meat and the unleavened bread. Fire flared from the rock, burning up the meat and the bread. And then the man vanished into thin air.

Dropping to his knees and hiding his face, Gideon exclaimed, "I've seen the angel of the Lord face to face! Sovereign Lord, spare me!"

"Fear not," came the Lord's voice. "Peace to you."

And so Gideon built an altar in that place, calling it The-Lord-Shalom, which means *the Lord is peace*.

Dig a Little Deeper

- Consider the meal Gideon offered. Why is giving harder when something is rare, costly, or scarce?

- Read Mark 12:41–44. Does God care how much you give or how you give? What do you have to offer?

- Why would God choose a man like Gideon (see Deut. 7:6–8 and 1 Cor. 1:27)?

A LITTLE LOWER

A Bible Lesson

> What are human beings that you think about
> them? What is a son of man that you take care of
> him? You made them a little lower than the angels.
> You placed on them a crown of glory and honor.
>
> —HEBREWS 2:6–7 (NIrV)

Hebrews 2:9 tells us that when Jesus came to earth, He was made a little lower than the angels for a while. He left heaven. He shed His glory. Paul talks about Jesus' unique abdication. Even though He was God, He "made himself nothing, by taking the very nature of a servant, being made in human likeness" (Phil. 2:7). This temporary change in status was righted at the resurrection, when Jesus defeated death and ascended back to heaven as rightful ruler over all beings.

But where do humans fit in line with angels?

God's Mighty Ones: In a way, angels have an advantage over us. They bore witness to creation. They inhabit God's throne room. They can see His glory firsthand. They have no need of faith because they stand in His presence and walk in His light.

Ministering Spirits: For humans, it's a different story. We must live by faith, obeying a God we cannot see. "Faith is being sure of what we hope for. It is being sure of what we do not see" (Heb. 11:1 NIrV). When we believe, God adopts us as His own children, and faith appears to boost humans up the heavenly hierarchy. "Are not all angels ministering spirits sent to serve those who will inherit salvation?" (Heb. 1:14). Paul even says that one day we'll judge angels (see 1 Cor. 6:3).

Fellow Servants: Whatever this responsibility means for us in the future, one thing is clear. Humans and angels are fellow servants (Rev. 22:9).

Dig a Little Deeper

- What does Jesus say about His servants in John 12:26?
- How do you serve others? What do you like about doing your part?
- What does Paul say in 1 Corinthians 14:12? And what perspective should we take, according to Ephesians 6:7?

Q. How do we know that the serpent in the Garden of Eden was the devil?

Q&A

> He seized the dragon, that ancient serpent, who is the devil, or Satan, and bound him for a thousand years.
>
> —Revelation 20:2

You know, that's a very good question, especially since the snake isn't unmasked in Genesis. He steps onto the scene as an animal of uncommon beauty and cleverness ... and slithers off again after his damage is done.

> Now the serpent was more crafty than any of the wild animals which the LORD God had made.
>
> —Genesis 3:1

He passes the time by chatting with Eve—charming and disarming. They talk gardening, and he brings up an interesting fact about the Tree of the Knowledge of Good and Evil. According to the serpent, one taste will bring her closer to her maker. She can be like God. But that's what Satan tried to do himself.

> O Lucifer ... you have said in your heart ... "I will ascend above the heights of the clouds, I will be like the Most High."
>
> —ISAIAH 14:12–14 (NKJV)

Curious. Convinced. Eve takes the serpent at his word, and she follows his lead. And so the fallen angel lures humanity into their own fall. Which brings us back to our original question. How do we know that the snake was Satan? Because the Bible confirms it. Genesis finds its echo in Revelation, where beginnings and endings collide.

> The great dragon was hurled down—that ancient serpent called the devil, or Satan, who leads the whole world astray. He was hurled to the earth, and his angels with him.
>
> —REVELATION 12:9

Dig a Little Deeper

- Why are lies so dangerous?
- Did you know God has a list of things He hates? What seven detestable things are listed in Proverbs 6:16–19?
- Read Philippians 4:8 and start a new list. What things please God?

OPEN HIS EYES

Meeting an Angel

Then the LORD opened the servant's eyes, and
he looked and saw the hills full of horses
and chariots of fire all around Elisha.

—2 KINGS 6:17

Elisha's servant lived in a perpetual state of awe, accompanied by a healthy dose of fear. His master was very particular when giving instructions. Messages had to be relayed word-for-word because Elisha spoke for God. Time and again, these messages had saved the lives of God's people. All to the frustration of the Arameans.

After setting Elisha's meal before him, the servant remarked, "The enemy is in a rage."

"The king of Aram thinks he has a spy amid his officers."

The servant filled his master's cup. "Perhaps they will turn on each other and leave us alone."

"No. God has shown me what's going on. The king is no longer suspicious; he knows for certain who has been exposing him."

That didn't sound good. "What has he learned?"

"The captains fell all over themselves, protesting their innocence," Elisha said. "Their king didn't believe them at first. But then an officer stepped forward."

"What did he say?"

With a small smile, Elisha adopted a quavering tone. "None of us, my lord the king—but Elisha, the prophet who is in Israel! He tells their king the very words you speak in your bedroom."

The servant gaped. But then he realized what Elisha's vision meant. "My lord, you are exposed. They will come for you!"

"Yes."

"But ... we have no protection here. We should flee!"

"No. We'll remain here."

When morning broke, the servant climbed to a vantage point in order to check the roads. If there was no sign of the enemy armies, he could at least prepare breakfast in peace. But the servant's heart turned to stone at the sight awaiting him.

Stumbling home, the young man panted, "Surrounded! All of it! The army of Aram is *here*!" He caught hold of his master's sleeve. "Oh, my lord, what will we do?"

Elisha patted his shoulder. "Don't be afraid. Those who are with us are more than those who are with them."

Who could remain calm at a time like this? "Dothan is besieged. They'll surely put us all to the sword!"

"No." And lifting his eyes to the sky, Elisha prayed, "O Lord, open his eyes. Let him see."

His servant gasped, for the sky blazed. Knees trembling, he climbed to the rooftop in order to better see the army of the Lord. Angel warriors filled the sky, and their horses and chariots blazed upon the surrounding hillsides. God was with Elisha. There truly was nothing to fear.

Dig a Little Deeper

- There's an old saying, "Seeing is believing." Why is seeing something firsthand so powerful?

- How much are you willing to take someone else's word for something. Can having someone say, "It'll be okay" be enough?

- If you could, would you want to see what Elisha saw? How would your life or faith change?

Q. Are there angels inside the ark of the covenant?

Q&A

> And you shall make two cherubim of gold;
> of hammered work you shall make them
> at the two ends of the mercy seat.
>
> —Exodus 25:18 (NKJV)

One of the most famous historical artifacts is the ark of the covenant. The ark has been made famous by movies, books, history buffs, and adventure seekers. The ark of the covenant is also called the ark of the testimony. It was fashioned from acacia wood and overlaid with hammered gold. The upper part of this precious box is called the mercy seat. Angels with outstretched wings face one another with heads bowed.

So who sits on the mercy seat? The short answer is God. "There I will meet with you, and I will speak with you from above the mercy seat, from between the two cherubim" (Ex. 25:22 NKJV). This is why the God of Israel came to be known as "the God who is enthroned between the cherubim."

We don't know where the ark is, but the Bible tells us what's inside.

Stone Tablets: The most famous items in the ark of the covenant are the stone tablets on which God wrote the Ten Commandments. Moses said, "I came back down the mountain and put the tablets in the ark I had made, as the LORD commanded me, and they are there now" (Deut. 10:5).

Jar of Manna: God commanded Moses to have a portion of manna placed inside the ark. "Keep it for generations to come, so they can see the bread I gave you to eat in the wilderness when I brought you out of Egypt" (Ex. 16:32).

Aaron's staff: In Numbers 16, Moses and Aaron had a mutiny on their hands. To settle it, God had them collect twelve staffs, one from each tribe. Their names were written on them, and they were placed in the Tabernacle. The next day, God made known His choice of leaders, for Aaron's staff had sprouted, budded, blossomed, and produced almonds. This miraculous staff was placed inside the ark of the covenant.

> Behind the second curtain was a room called the Most Holy Place, which had the golden altar of incense and the gold-covered ark of the covenant. This ark contained the gold jar of manna, Aaron's staff that had budded, and the stone tablets of the covenant. Above the ark were the cherubim of the Glory, overshadowing the atonement cover.
>
> —HEBREWS 9:3–5

Dig a Little Deeper

- Do you keep souvenirs from trips? Do you have mementos from life-changing events? Why do we accumulate and keep these things?

- What are some remembrances God established in Genesis 9:13, Exodus 31:18, Joshua 4:6–7, and Luke 22:19?

- What is promised to overcomers in Revelation 2:17?

Don't Look Back

Meeting an Angel

> With the coming of dawn, the angels
> urged Lot, saying, "Hurry!"
> —Genesis 19:15

Hurry! Take your wife and daughters or you'll all be swept away!"

"Swept away," muttered Lot's wife. These two were the ones doing all the sweeping! Perfect strangers, yet they'd strolled into their home and made a mess of things. She was sick of their high and mighty act. What gave them the right to hand down orders? And her husband hadn't stopped bowing since they'd arrived. "You watch. It's a joke, just like my sons-in-law say."

"They're *angels*, my dove," Lot said in urgent tones. "Messengers from God!"

"Messengers should have better manners," she groused. "They have insulted our family, our friends, our very way of life!"

Her husband pulled anxiously at his beard. "My uncle would do as they say. We should listen."

She grumbled and complained, but she kept packing. If this was a scam to lure them away from home so thieves could overturn their household, she wouldn't leave anything more than trifles.

All night she heaped and sorted, so that by the time Lot finally pushed her through their back door and into the street, she could barely move under her burden. Her daughters also carried heavy bundles.

She was mentally reviewing the things she'd need to buy when the angels started in again. Taking her hand, one of them pulled her along, hurrying her steps. "The city will be punished. Flee to the mountains! Flee for your lives! Don't look back!"

"The mountains!" she squeaked in outrage. "Do you expect me to abandon our fine home and scrabble in the wilderness?"

Lot gave her a pained look, but he took her side. "Please my lords. The road into the mountains is too steep. The disaster you mentioned would overtake us before we reached safety. If I've found any favor in your sight, give us an easier way."

The two men traded a long look, but they said nothing.

Casting about, Lot pointed to a dingy little town on the very edge of the plain. "There for example!" he suggested. "Zoar is nearer, and it's a small place. Let us go there, so my life will be spared."

"Very well," said one of the angels. "God will hold back His judgment until you reach the town. Now run! And don't look back!"

The road may have been easier, but it was still longer than she liked. Struggling and stewing, the woman kept up her inner tirade against her foolhardy husband, the haughty angels, and the unreasonable God of Abraham, who had no business meddling with her comfort, her position, and her daughters' futures.

Heedless of every warning, she stopped walking. Lot's wife turned away from mercy and found the end of God's patience. That one look was her last.

But Lot's wife looked back, and she became a pillar of salt.

—Genesis 19:26

Dig a Little Deeper

- When is it harder to obey: when you're told to do something or when you're told not to do something? Why?

- What kinds of things do you do because they're "for your own good," not because you want to do them?

- Have you ever had to leave something or someone behind? How did you feel?

Q. WILL THERE BE ANIMALS IN HEAVEN?

Q&A

> I saw heaven standing open and there before me was a white horse, whose rider is called Faithful and True.
>
> —REVELATION 19:11

Strangely enough, the number one question I'm asked by young readers isn't about angels. (But my answer is!) They often ask if there will be animals in heaven. Yep, I think so! At the very least, there'll be horses. And they are often accompanied by angels.

> As they were walking along and talking together, suddenly a chariot of fire and horses of fire appeared and separated the two of them, and Elijah went up to heaven in a whirlwind.
>
> —2 KINGS 2:11

> Then the LORD opened the servant's eyes, and he looked and saw the hills full of horses and chariots of fire all around Elisha.
>
> —2 KINGS 6:17

> There before me was a man mounted on a red horse
> ... Behind him were red, brown and white horses.
>
> —ZECHARIAH 1:8

> The armies of heaven were following him, riding on
> white horses and dressed in fine linen, white and clean.
>
> —REVELATION 19:14

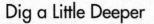

Dig a Little Deeper

- Why do you think so many people want to know about animals in heaven?
- What do John 1:1–5 and Colossians 1:16 teach us about Jesus' role in Creation?
- What do we know about heaven from Revelation 21:4–5?

GLORY TO GOD

A Bible Lesson

> The heavenly host appeared ... praising God and saying, "Glory to God in the highest heaven, and on earth peace to those on whom his favor rests."
>
> —LUKE 2:13–14

Christians talk about the glory of God, and we know that angels glorify Him. But what does that mean?

First of all, glory generally means awesomeness, brilliance, or beauty. Those words definitely apply to God. But God's glory also means God's presence. Second, glory was something the Israelites could see. A shining cloud. One that marked God's presence among His people. This cloud led the children of Israel through the wilderness (see Ex. 13:21). God's glory also came down as fire and smoke, surrounding Mt. Sinai when God met Moses there (see Ex. 19:18). It also appeared at the dedication of Solomon's temple.

> When the priests withdrew from the Holy Place, the cloud filled the temple of the LORD. And the priests could not perform their service because of the cloud, for the glory of the LORD filled his temple.
>
> —1 KINGS 8:10–11

So what does it mean to glorify God? We can't add to His perfection, but believers can bring attention to God's glory by reflecting it. How? According to the Bible, that's mostly done *out loud!*

And Mary said: "My soul glorifies the Lord and my spirit rejoices in God my Savior."

—Luke 1:46–47

So when the centurion saw what had happened, he glorified God, saying, "Certainly this was a righteous Man!"

—Luke 23:47 (NKJV)

To him who sits on the throne and to the Lamb be praise and honor and glory and power, for ever and ever!

—Revelation 5:13

Whoever offers praise glorifies Me; and to him who orders *his* conduct *aright* I will show the salvation of God.

—Psalm 50:23 (NKJV)

For you were bought at a price; therefore glorify God in your body and in your spirit, which are God's.

—1 Corinthians 6:20 (NKJV)

Say it. Sing it. Shine it. Be a light, and live in a way that will lead others to the God who deserves all the glory.

Dig a Little Deeper

- What's the difference between glorifying God in your body and in your spirit? How do those two things fit together?
- Read Isaiah 42:8. What's God's opinion about glory?
- What are some other words for glory? Have you heard the phrase "glory hog"? How do people grasp at glory for themselves?

THE ANGEL OF HIS PRESENCE

Meeting an Angel

See, I am sending an angel ahead of
you to guard you along the way.

—EXODUS 23:20

Aaron stood by while Moses lifted his voice. Even though Aaron had spoken for his brother in Egypt and their early days in the wilderness, Moses had brought down God's commands from the mountaintop. He was different. Somehow radiant. So much more comfortable in front of the crowd.

His words rang out. "My angel will guard you along the way and bring you to the place I have prepared. Pay attention to him! Listen to what he says! He has my name!"

The angel of God had been traveling with them, first leading, then following as constant as the cloud that billowed overhead (see Ex. 14:19). Their guide and guard, providing shade from the unrelenting sun. Cool breezes by day. Warmth and light through the night. Fire flickered in that twisting column, making it possible to journey through the night. Never in darkness, the Israelites lived in the shadow of God's presence. He marked their steps, leading them like a flock, keeping the promise He'd made to their forefathers—and now to them.

> In all their distress he too was distressed, and the angel of his presence saved them. In his love and mercy he redeemed them; he lifted them up and carried them all the days of old.
>
> —Isaiah 63:9

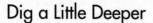

Dig a Little Deeper

- Given what we know about the Angel of the Lord, who may have been walking with Moses through the wilderness?

- When did the Lord and His friend Moses find the time for another chat? Check Matthew 17:3.

- What do we learn about Moses' death in Deuteronomy 34:5–6? Because of the wording in Jude 1:9, tradition holds that which angel buried Moses?

Q. WHY DID SOME OF THE ANGELS FALL?

Q&A

> I saw Satan fall like lightning from heaven.
> —LUKE 10:18

Angels stand in God's presence, see His face, hear His voice. Heaven is their home, yet some turned their backs on paradise. Following Satan, they were driven from heaven and became demons. But *why*? The Bible gives us a glimpse of the attitudes that contributed to these angels' downfall.

Conceit: When Paul wrote about the qualifications for pastors, he told Timothy, "He must not be a recent convert, or he may become conceited and fall under the same judgment as the devil" (1 Tim. 3:6).

Lies: Jesus was quite blunt in His assessment of Satan. "When he lies, he speaks his native language, for he is a liar and the father of lies" (John 8:44).

Wickedness: Jesus referred to Satan as "the evil one" (Matt. 13:19). And in the passage that describes the fall of Satan, the prophet said, "You were blameless in your ways from the day you were created till wickedness was found in you" (Ezek. 28:15).

Violence: The same prophet accused Satan of violence in his dealings. "Through your widespread trade you were filled with violence" (Ezek. 28:16).

Vanity: More traits emerge in this passage. "Your heart became proud on account of your beauty, and you corrupted your wisdom because of your splendor" (Ezek. 28:17).

Desecration: Although no specifics are given, this angel's guilt piled up. "By your many sins and dishonest trade you have desecrated your sanctuaries" (Ezek. 28:18).

Murder: The devil is ruthless indeed, for Jesus said, "He was a murderer from the beginning" (John 8:44).

All of these things happened *before* Satan and a third of the angels were cast from heaven, so this is a relatively short list. Ever since then, the enemy has continued to oppose God, working to thwart divine plans. But it's no use. As the writer of Hebrews pointed out, Jesus came and died "so that by his death he might break the power of him who holds the power of death—that is, the devil" (Heb. 2:14).

Why did the angels fall? The simplest answer is because they sinned.

Dig a Little Deeper

- A fallen angel may have orchestrated the fall of humanity and murdered the Messiah, but his triumph was short-lived. How did God turn the tables according to Colossians 2:15?

- Eve wasn't the only person Satan deceived. According to Luke 22:3 and John 13:27, who else did the devil lure into sin?

- One of the devil's nicknames is *Accuser*. What do we see him doing in Zechariah 3:1?

IN YOUR NAME

A Bible Lesson

> When Jesus had called the Twelve together,
> he gave them power and authority to drive
> out all demons and to cure diseases.
>
> —LUKE 9:1

Two-by-two, Jesus had sent out His disciples, and two-by-two, they returned. John was one of the first to arrive at the meeting place, and he chose a seat close to Jesus. The more disciples who showed up, the greater the noise. John leaned over and remarked, "The seventy-two have returned with joy."

Jesus asked, "Do you understand why?"

The reason seemed obvious, but John enjoyed sorting out individual threads of conversation from the hubbub. Before long, he realized there was a common theme. In a low voice, he ventured, "I think it's because we were able to do so much."

Jesus called the crowd to order. "What do you have to report?"

"It was amazing!" exclaimed one man. "Lord, even the demons submit to us in your name!"

More of the men offered testimonies. Healings. Miracles. Power. Jesus' name carried weight in the supernatural realm, and all seventy-two were heady with triumph.

As soon as Jesus began speaking, a hush fell over them. "I saw Satan fall like lightning from heaven. I've given you authority to trample on snakes and scorpions and to overcome all the power of the enemy; nothing will harm you. *However* ..." He waited for the murmurs to dwindle before continuing. "Don't rejoice that the spirits submit to you. Instead, rejoice that your names are written in heaven."

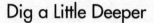

Dig a Little Deeper

- Have you ever started taking a test, only to realize you studied all the wrong things? Can it be hard to figure out what's most important?

- If you could perform miracles, how would you use your power?

- What was Jesus' purpose in giving the disciples power over demons (see 1 Pet. 4:11)?

THE STUBBORN DONKEY

Meeting an Angel

Then the angel of the LORD stood in a narrow path
through the vineyards, with walls on both sides.

—NUMBERS 22:24

Balaam was a man whose words were said to impress the gods.
If he pronounced a blessing, that man was blessed. And if he
pronounced a curse, that man was cursed. Since his track record
was flawless, he could charge high prices. But when a royal del-
egation arrived to hire him to put a curse on Israel, Balaam was
caught between the king of Moab and the God of Israel.

"How do you refuse someone who won't take *no* for an
answer?" he muttered under his breath.

"Sir?"

Waving off his servant, Balaam complained, "The king's
offer is rich. His wealth could be mine. Yet I must offend him.
Can the spokesman of God speak what's been forbidden by God?"

"Will you take the side of Israel?"

Balaam's frown took a sulky turn. "I am on no side but my
own. There *must* be a way to turn this to my advantage."

"You'll think of something, sir," his servant said. "You
always do."

If so, it needed to be soon. Balaam smacked his donkey's
flank and growled, "Let's get this over with."

With an oily smile for the Moabite officials who were his escort, Balaam silently wracked his brain. Perhaps he could say something that was both ominous and harmless? His stomach churned. His tongue grew heavy. And Balaam's temper grew as short as the prickling hair on his donkey's neck.

That's when his trusty mount veered right off the road. By the time Balaam beat her back onto the road, his face was flushed with embarrassment and anger, for his royal escorts were laughing at him.

When the road narrowed between two vineyards, she did it again, trotting sideways and crushing his foot against the wall. Balaam's roar of pain earned him everyone's attention, and his fury exploded.

"Perhaps you should curse the donkey and be done with her!" taunted one of the Moabites.

The donkey bucked and turned in circles then dropped to the ground under her master. Balaam's humiliation was complete. Limping and cursing, he turned on her with his staff. He might have bludgeoned the life from her stubborn frame, but the beast laid back her ears and brayed her protest *in words* that sent ice down Balaam's spine.

"What did I ever do to you? Why do I deserve these beatings?"

"You've made a fool of me!" he blustered. "I'd kill you now if I had a sword!"

Rolling her eyes back, she said, "Am I not your own donkey? Am I in the habit of disobeying you?"

"No!" Balaam glanced around to see if anyone else could understand her words. And that's when he saw it. A mighty angel stood in the road, sword drawn. Immediately, Balaam dropped to the dirt. "I didn't realize!"

The angel's answer let the prophet know how close to death he'd come.

I have come here to oppose you because your path is a reckless one before me. The donkey saw me and turned away from me these three times. If it had not turned away, I would certainly have killed you by now, but I would have spared it.

—Numbers 22:32–33

Dig a Little Deeper

- What usually happens when you lose your temper?
- How did God use the donkey in this story to further His kingdom?
- If God can use a donkey, how do you think He will use you?

Q. Do angels play harps?

Q&A

> The sound I heard was like the
> music of harps being played.
> —Revelation 14:2 (NIrV)

In art, it's easy to pick an angel out of the crowd. He's the one with the ankle-length nightie and the pure white wings of a dove. And his accessories are equally telltale—a golden halo hovering over his head and a harp tucked in the crook of his arm. But do angels really play harps?

A quick check of the scriptures verifies that harps and heaven really do go together. John says, "And I heard a sound from heaven like the roar of rushing waters and like a loud peal of thunder. The sound I heard was like that of harpists playing their harps" (Rev. 14:2). But we can't exactly point to this verse as proof of an angelic orchestra. In the first place, this passage isn't even about angels. And in the second, John says the sound was *like* harps.

Throughout the book of Revelation, John is struggling to describe the marvels of heaven by comparing them to things we understand. It would be like me trying to explain a peacock to you by saying, "he was a splendid chicken, having a hundred eyes and crowned with sapphires." He paints a vivid picture, but we have to realize that words can fall short, especially when describing the indescribable.

Harps are mentioned again in Revelation 15:2: "Then I saw something that looked like a sea of glass glowing with fire. Standing beside the sea were those who had won the battle over the beast. They had also overcome its statue and the number of its name. They held harps given to them by God" (NIrV).

Aha! So we know that there will be some kind of stringed instrument in heaven, and these harps are gifts from God. But the interesting thing is that in this verse, it's *not* angels who play them. They're given to the victorious, who then sing the song of the Lamb.

Dig a Little Deeper

- What are some of the lyrics for the song of the Lamb, as found in Revelation 15:3–4?
- What songs would you include in the soundtrack for a big celebration?
- Read 1 Samuel 16:18. Why did Saul call for David?

RUNNING INTERFERENCE
A Bible Lesson

> Like a snow-cooled drink at harvest time is a
> trustworthy messenger to the one who sends
> him; he refreshes the spirit of his master.
>
> —PROVERBS 25:13

Daniel turned at the sudden rush of wind and clatter of falling scrolls, only to find an angel collapsed on his floor. Battered and barely standing, this servant of God looked like something the cat dragged in. Mustering a weary sort of dignity, the angel staggered to his feet and said, "I was detained."

This wasn't the first time he saw an angel. In the book of Daniel, we encounter hints of angelic combat. Gabriel arrives "in swift flight about the time of the evening sacrifice" (Dan. 9:21). Heaven's messengers aren't speedy without reason. Angels encounter obstacles, ambushes, and other assorted perils. Another time, an angelic messenger reaches the prophet, but only after a three-week delay. The enemy resisted and kept him from getting to Daniel. This angel needed to be rescued by Michael.

> The prince of the Persian kingdom resisted me twenty-one days. Then Michael, one of the chief princes, came to help me, because I was detained there with the king of Persia.
>
> —DANIEL 10:13

This is part of the warfare in the supernatural realm. Spiritual battles take place all around us, with God's servants fighting on our behalf.

Dig a Little Deeper

- Angels have struggles and difficulties. How does that change your perspective on them?
- Let's switch things around. If you could have an angel carry a message to heaven's throne room, what would you have him say to God?
- How can you join the battle (see Eph. 6:10–17)?

Q. IS THERE ANY CHANCE I'LL EVER GET TO SEE A REAL LIVE ANGEL?

Q&A

This will happen when the Lord Jesus
is revealed from heaven in blazing
fire with his powerful angels.

—2 THESSALONIANS 1:7

Yes, your chances are excellent. In fact, I'm one hundred percent sure you'll be feasting your eyes on heaven's hosts someday. Because when Jesus comes again, He's not coming alone. Consider the promises that these verses hold.

For the Son of Man is going to come in his Father's
glory with his angels.

—MATTHEW 16:27

When the Son of Man comes in his glory, and all the
angels with him, he will sit on his glorious throne.

—MATTHEW 25:31

... when he comes in his Father's glory with the holy
angels.

—MARK 8:38

This will happen when the Lord Jesus is revealed from heaven in blazing fire with his powerful angels.

—2 Thessalonians 1:7

And he will send his angels with a loud trumpet call, and they will gather his elect from the four winds, from one end of the heavens to the other.

—Matthew 24:31

Were you hoping to see an angel sooner? Well, there's always a chance, but remember the encouragement of Hebrews 13:2. "Do not forget to show hospitality to strangers, for by so doing some people have shown hospitality to angels without knowing it." The Bible says you might very well meet an angel one day ... without being aware of it. So be kind and encourage those you meet. Who knows? An angel may be holding onto his *thank you* for when you meet up in heaven.

Dig a Little Deeper

- God will come for us when the time is right, and in the twinkling of an eye, everything will change. Do you feel prepared for that at-any-moment call?

- Read Matthew 25:1–13. What does Jesus say about being ready for His return?

- How can we go about making the most of every opportunity (see Eph. 5:15–17) between now and soon?

FACING THE FURNACE

Meeting an Angel

Nebuchadnezzar said, "Praise be to the God
of Shadrach, Meshach and Abednego, who
has sent his angel and rescued his servants!"

—DANIEL 3:28

Shadrach, Meshach, and Abednego remained strong before the king. Even Nebuchadnezzar's fury wasn't enough to shake their hearts or minds. Nothing on earth could drive them to bow before a false god. And in standing tall while every other man and woman lowered themselves, these three Hebrews had condemned themselves in the eyes of the king.

"O, Nebuchadnezzar, we won't defend ourselves to you," Shadrach said. "If we're thrown into the blazing furnace, the God we serve is able to save us."

Abednego continued, "But even if He doesn't rescue us from your hand, we want you to know, O king. We'll never serve your gods or worship the golden statue you set up."

And so despite their years of faithful service to both the king and his empire, Nebuchadnezzar ordered the furnace to be stoked. Even though they didn't struggle, ropes were brought. Before the entire court, the three were bound hand and foot and carried out of the king's presence. The men who hated them cheered and cast insults, heaping shame on their heads. But Shadrach, Meshach, and Abednego didn't beg for mercy or lose their resolve.

Seven times hotter than usual, the furnace's heat made the lower chamber of the palace a hell. Flames roared. Metal glowed. Men sweated.

Meshach whispered, "This is madness. The heat of the king's fury will turn his palace to ash."

"And those within it," agreed Abednego in somber tones. Looking into the face of his captor, he urged, "Unbind our feet, or you'll carry us to your death."

Relief flashed through the soldier's eyes, but then the king roared, "Bring them! Cast them in!"

Stokers hurried forward to open the furnace doors. The blast of heat they released seared their flesh, killing them instantly. Meshach groaned. "Tell me this is a bad dream."

"It's not," Shadrach said, his voice oddly calm in the midst of horrors. "But I see a man in the furnace, and I know him from dreams."

Abednego twisted around, trying to see for himself. "Where?"

With a soft gasp, Meshach said, "He's there, and his arms are open."

"Will this angel lead us to heaven?" Abednego asked.

"If the king has his way," Shadrach replied. "But I am certain that God will have *His* way in this matter."

Dig a Little Deeper

- How would you have responded to the king's judgment?
- Do you think you could hang onto faith in the face of such terrible persecution? How can this help you appreciate your religious freedom?
- What does Job 12:9–10 tell us about God?

BROTHERS AND SISTERS

A Bible Lesson

There is rejoicing in the presence of the angels
of God over one sinner who repents.

—LUKE 15:10

Families are fascinating, flexible things. We're mixed, blended, and amended with steps and halves, greats and grands, in-laws and extendeds. Fathers and daughters. Mothers and sons. It's only natural! But love can bind humans together in ways that are stronger than blood ties. Newlyweds strike out and start their own families. Adoptive parents welcome someone else's children into their hearts and homes. Good neighbors can be closer than kin.

In a similar way, believers are connected. Only instead of blood ties, we have Jesus in common. He claims us as His own. "Then he looked at those seated in a circle around him and said, 'Here are my mother and my brothers!'" (Mark 3:34). Children of God. Heirs to eternity. Members of the Beloved.

By faith, we join God's family, becoming sons and daughters of God (see Gal. 3:26) and co-heirs with Jesus (see Rom. 8:17). As the firstborn of God, He's our big brother. And heaven celebrates each new addition to the family. Jesus tells us, "There is rejoicing in the presence of the angels of God over one sinner who repents" (Luke 15:10).

Let's back up a moment and make sure that's clear, because it's important.

Q. Who are sinners?

A. We all are. Imperfect from the very start of our lives, we carry on the legacy of the fall in the Garden of Eden.

Q. What does it mean to repent?

A. Repentance is more than saying sorry. Not only do we admit we're in the wrong, but we also turn from our sin and walk a new way. A change of heart shows up in how we live.

Q. Why do the angels care?

A. God's plan for redemption wowed the heavens to such a degree that they can't tear their eyes away. They're "ministering servants sent to serve those who will inherit salvation" (Heb. 1:14), so they're paying attention to each new member of God's family.

You might be wondering how the angels find out about our salvation. After all, don't they hang out in heaven? Consider this. In Zephaniah 3:17, the prophet says, "The LORD your God is with you. He is the Mighty Warrior who saves. He will take great delight in you. In his love he will no longer punish you. Instead, he will sing for joy because of you" (NIrV). Did you catch that? *God* is singing about you!

The God who knows everything definitely knows when a new son or daughter joins His family. If there's a party in the heavens, He's the one who kicks it off, leading the heavenly chorus in songs of welcome.

Dig a Little Deeper

- What does your family look like? Who's included?
- How can you treat Christian friends as family?
- Who do you know that you'd love to see again in heaven? You could even include favorite actors, authors, and musicians on your list. Will you commit to praying for them?

Q. Is Satan a Fallen Angel?

Q&A

> Then war broke out in heaven. Michael and his angels fought against the dragon, and the dragon and his angels fought back.
>
> —Revelation 12:7

Yes, and he appears to be the leader of other angels who were cast out of heaven (see Rev. 12:7). And they are at war with heaven. Satan is called by several names throughout the scriptures—Lucifer, the devil, the deceiver, the accuser, and even the dragon.

Many people consider Lucifer to be this enemy's "official" name, which means "star" or "light bringer." It's interesting to point out that this is his Latin name. In Hebrew, the angel's name was *Helel*, which means "brilliant one."

Here are a few verses that have shaped our impressions of this fallen angel.

> How you are fallen from heaven, O Lucifer, son of the morning! *How* you are cut down to the ground, you who weakened the nations! For you have said in your heart: "I will ascend into heaven, I will exalt my throne above the stars of God; I will also sit on the mount of the congregation on the farthest sides of the north; I will ascend above the heights of the clouds, I will be like the Most High."
>
> —Isaiah 14:12–14 (NKJV)

The great dragon was hurled down—that ancient serpent called the devil, or Satan, who leads the whole world astray. He was hurled to the earth, and his angels with him.

—Revelation 12:9

You belong to your father, the devil, and you want to carry out your father's desires. He was a murderer from the beginning, not holding to the truth, for there is no truth in him. When he lies, he speaks his native language, for he is a liar and the father of lies.

—John 8:44

One day the angels came to present themselves before the Lord, and Satan also came with them. The Lord said to Satan, "Where have you come from?"

Satan answered the Lord, "From roaming through the earth and going back and forth on it."

—Job 1:6–7

While we don't want to give undue attention to this fallen angel, we need to be smart. Know your enemy. Be wise to his tricks. And resist the devil's temptations (see James 4:7).

Dig a Little Deeper

- Why do you think people are often fascinated by the villain in a story? Why do bad guys have an appeal?
- What is the principle in James 4:7?
- Take a look at Zechariah 3:1. If we were on trial for our lives, what would Satan's role be in heaven's courtroom? What is Jesus' role (see 1 John 2:1)?

I SAW THE LORD

Meeting an Angel

Then one of the seraphim flew to me,
having in his hand a live coal *which* he
had taken with the tongs from the altar.

—ISAIAH 6:6 (NKJV)

Isaiah's heart beat so wildly that he was sure it would stop. If this was a dream, he couldn't fathom its basis. Rainbow light and crystal splendor. Winged creatures filled the air, beating at sweet-smelling smoke. Flames blazed upon an altar, and above all else rose a lofty throne. And when he lifted his eyes, Isaiah saw the Lord. The train of His robes filled the temple.

With knees like water, Isaiah made himself small as he listened to the seraphim call out to one another. "Holy, holy, holy is the Lord Almighty; the whole earth is full of His glory!" Their voices were so loud that they shook the throne room.

Could he join them? How could he, being a sinful man? Cowering in dismay, the prophet exclaimed, "Woe to me! I'm ruined!"

One of the seraphim flew to the altar. Hovering there for several moments, he turned and glided to where Isaiah trembled. Upon seeing what he carried, the prophet's stomach dropped. With a pair of tongs, the angel had brought a coal from the altar. It sparked and glowed. With a rustle of feathers, the angel loomed closer, and Isaiah shuddered in fear. But his fellow servant took the ember in his hands, reverently cradling the fiery fragment without being burned. So Isaiah held his ground, and the angel came closer. No heat. No fear. And no question what he must do. The touch was like a kiss.

"See, this has touched your lips," said the seraphim. "Your guilt is taken away, and your sin atoned for!"

Wonderment and awe turned to hope as the voice of the Lord filled the throne room. "Whom shall I send? And who will go for us?"

"Me!" Isaiah lifted his arms and called out, "Here am I! Send me!"

Dig a Little Deeper

- What did Isaiah mean when he called himself a man of unclean lips?

- What does Jesus say in Matthew 15:8 about our words? How did David pray in Psalm 19:14?

- Have you ever volunteered for anything? What will you say when God calls you to do something for Him?

DOCTRINE OF ANGELS
A Bible Lesson

His face like lightning, his eyes like flaming torches, his arms and legs like the gleam of burnished bronze, and his voice like the sound of a multitude.

—DANIEL 10:6

You can make a study of angels. There are reference books and commentaries to help you along. Each volume neatly lists their supernatural traits and discusses their roles in God's master plan. Angels are neatly filed away under their own theological subheading—angelology. Their existence is scrupulously documented, cross-referenced, and footnoted in biblical history, rabbinical tradition, and academic research.

These rigorous academic works are often hard to read. And not simply because they're full of lofty words and ancient languages. They may be a faithful record of the biblical passages in which angels appear, but they lack personality. It's like trying to get a sense of humanity by skimming through the contact list on a stranger's phone. Names and numbers. An email address. Maybe a birthday. But people are more than information. And angels are too.

When men and women met them, they probably jumped and made undignified yelps and squeaks. Hearts raced. Knees wobbled. Grown men fainted. Kings hid. Prophets begged for their lives.

Only a small part of their story is handed down to us. But it's enough for us to know that they're not nameless, faceless beings.

They're more than words in a textbook. Angels are individuals with personalities. They have jobs to do, choices to make, and risks to take. Our curiosity about them is only natural.

Mere words fall short when it comes to humans, angels, heaven, and especially to God himself. If everything were written down, "the whole world would not have room for the books that would be written" (John 21:25). All of which means we have so much to look forward to!

> It is written: "What no eye has seen, what no ear has heard, and what no human mind has conceived"—the things God has prepared for those who love him— these are the things God has revealed to us by His Spirit.
>
> —1 CORINTHIANS 2:9–10A

Dig a Little Deeper

- Can you think of a time when words failed you? When is it hardest to express what's in your heart or on your mind?

- Everything in the Bible is true. But everything isn't in the Bible. According to 2 Peter 1:3–4, what does the Bible give us?

- Go to Hebrews 4:12 and 1 Peter 1:23. Why is God's Word different from anyone else's writing?

Q. IS THERE SUCH A THING AS AN ANGEL OF DEATH?

Q&A

> And the LORD sent an angel, who annihilated all the fighting men and the commanders and officers in the camp of the Assyrian king.
>
> —2 CHRONICLES 32:21

No. This is a human legend, found in many cultures. Creative storytellers have made death into a person. In Anglo-Saxon tradition, this fictional figure is called the Grim Reaper because he carries a scythe that he uses to sever a person's ties to this world. Stories have cropped up over the years about meeting death, outwitting death, and even keeping an appointment with death.

So are there biblical parallels that inspired this allegorical reaper? Certainly! Time and again, we see angels wreaking holy havoc. Look at these examples of death and disaster.

> When the angel stretched out his hand to destroy Jerusalem, the LORD relented concerning the disaster and said to the angel who was afflicting the people, "Enough! Withdraw your hand."
>
> —2 SAMUEL 24:16

> That night, the angel of the LORD went out and put to death a hundred and eighty-five thousand in the Assyrian camp. When the people got up the next morning—there were all the dead bodies!
>
> —2 KINGS 19:35

> Immediately, because Herod did not give praise to God, an angel of the Lord struck him down, and he was eaten by worms and died.
>
> —ACTS 12:23

Angels can be an instrument of judgment. And that's not necessarily a bad thing. Heaven's armies often had a hand in miraculous victories when His children were outnumbered and outgunned, they still came out on top. And God received the glory.

Dig a Little Deeper

- Why would the same angels who bring "glad tidings of great joy" also be called upon to bring death and judgment?
- If you could "outwit" death and live Methuselah's lifespan (969 years) on this earth, would you? Why?

THE HOUR IS NEAR

Meeting an Angel

An angel from heaven appeared
to him and strengthened him.

—LUKE 22:43

One last time. A final chance to do the usual thing. Knowing His time was near made each moment precious. The Lord couldn't—*wouldn't*—slow them down, but He could make the most of them. "Peter," Jesus called. "James, John, I'm going to pray."

"Wait for us."

They'd made him promise not to go off alone. Not with so much unrest in the city. The religious leaders had tried to corner Jesus more than once, so His friends were acting as bodyguards. If only they understood that Pharisees were the least of His worries. A much older, craftier enemy was at work.

As they wended their way between olive trees, Jesus remarked, "A sword doesn't suit you."

"*You* know it's a bluff, but troublemakers may think twice."

Choosing a quiet corner, Jesus called a halt. "Wait for me here. And pray."

John caught at his sleeve and asked, "What's wrong, Teacher? You look troubled."

"I am," Jesus replied. "My soul is overwhelmed with sorrow to the point of death. Stay close. Keep watch. And pray."

The three traded anxious glances. "We're here," said Peter.

"Don't worry about anything," said James.

Jesus was only a stone's throw away, so he heard Peter's snores. Picking His way back to His would-be guards, Jesus shook their shoulders. "It hasn't even been an hour. I thought you were going to watch and pray."

"Sorry," groaned Peter.

James sat up and punched his brother's shoulder. John got up and hurried forward. Touching Jesus' clammy cheek, he begged, "Forgive us."

"The spirit is willing, but the body is weak." Jesus shook His head. "Watch and pray."

But their eyes were heavy, and they were as exhausted as He was. While Jesus wrestled with His Father in prayer, the sounds of slumber came from His friends again. He prayed more earnestly, but anguish gripped His heart. Was there no other way? Could He withstand the horrors awaiting? Must He face them completely alone?

"I am here."

Jesus lifted His face and gazed into the bright countenance of a friend. The angel was as troubled as His disciples to see God tremble. But He brought words of comfort. Prophecies and promises as old as time. Whispers of hope. And with each reminder, the angel gave Jesus the strength He needed. For the hour had come. The Son of Man would be betrayed. It was time to suffer.

Dig a Little Deeper

- What good things do you try to make last as long as possible?

- When do you find yourself dragging your feet? What are the everyday things that you dread?

- How does Hebrews 12:2 say Jesus was able to face death on a cross?

Q. ARE ANGELS UNIQUE TO CHRISTIANITY?

Q&A

> They sacrificed to false gods, which are not God—gods they had not known, gods that recently appeared, gods your ancestors did not fear.
>
> —DEUTERONOMY 32:17

Nope. Angels in one form or another are found in nearly every religion on earth. But how they are viewed varies from faith to faith.

Honored: In some cultures, they're the servants and messengers of gods, and in others, they're treated like gods. They've been given names, ranks, and realms of influence. People worship them for their power and pray to them for protection. Paul said people who chase after the sensational and supernatural "are puffed up with idle notions by their unspiritual mind" (Col. 2:18).

Borrowed: Since there's plenty of drama in the standoff between angels and demons, they have universal appeal. It's not unusual to find angels lumped in with other supernatural or mythological beings. Therefore, they make excellent fodder for stories loosely based on Christian mythology. Fictional angels usually bear little resemblance to the servants of God found in the Bible.

Ignored: For some people, angels are out of sight, out of mind. They don't really have a part to play in everyday life, so why bother with them? Or sometimes their existence is called into question. In Paul's day, angels were the subject of theological debates. "The Sadducees say that there is no resurrection, and that there are neither angels nor spirits, but the Pharisees believe all these things" (Acts 23:8).

Variations of angels may appear around the world, but they're spin-offs and inventions. In some cases, they may be fallen angels who've set themselves up as gods (see Deut. 32:17). But these twists and turns will never cancel out the truth. Yes, angels are awesome and awe-inspiring. And like them, we worship only God.

Dig a Little Deeper

- Why do you think angels are so popular? Why are you interested in them?

- How much of what you hear about angels matches what the Bible says about them?

- What if angels were eager to talk to you one day? What questions do you think they might have for you?

THE HEAVENS WERE OPENED

Meeting an Angel

> In the fire was what looked like four living
> creatures. In appearance their form was human,
> but each of them had four faces and four wings.
>
> —EZEKIEL 1:5–6

I saw visions of God. Strange. Terrible. Awesome. But the Lord's hand was on me, so I looked at everything He showed me. At His word, the heavens were opened, and I searched for words to describe their wonders. Creatures with four faces. Dancing fire. A shining cloud.

How can I explain such wonders? There is nothing like them on earth, yet four stood before me. "Each of the four had the face of a human being, and on the right side each had the face of a lion, and on the left the face of an ox; each also had the face of an eagle" (Ezek. 1:10). These living creatures had four wings, calves' feet, and bodies that shone like polished bronze. And they moved at speeds that rival lightning flashing across the sky. Dancing like fire, they moved as God bid.

Near to these creatures, I saw wheels that sparkled like gems. "Their rims were high and awesome, and all four rims were full of eyes all around" (Ezek. 1:18). Wheels within wheels. A crystal expanse. A sapphire throne.

And then I saw a man surrounded by light. "I saw that from what appeared to be his waist up he looked like glowing metal, as if full of fire, and that from there down he looked like fire" (Ezek. 1:27). I gawked, searching for details to remember, but when God spoke, I fell on my face. Who can stand before His glory?

———————

Ezekiel's descriptions of heaven are some of the most vivid. What a wide (and somewhat wild) variety of living creatures! They're unlike anything I've seen in creation. These are some of the inhabitants of heaven. One day, they may be your neighbors!

Dig a Little Deeper

- What are some of the strangest, most wonderful parts of God's creation—animals, birds, insects, fish? Could you have imagined them?

- What do Job 5:9 and Psalm 40:5 say about God's ability to boggle the mind?

- Mysteries and miracles are a part of who God is. What does Psalm 78:4 say we should do about them?

AMEN AND AMEN
A Bible Lesson

All the angels were standing around the throne and around the elders and the four living creatures. They fell down on their faces before the throne and worshiped God, saying: "Amen! Praise and glory and wisdom and thanks and honor and power and strength be to our God for ever and ever. Amen!"

—REVELATION 7:11–12

The angels and elders in heaven call out, listing a bunch of things that belong to God. Take a look at all the stuff we owe Him.

Praise: "The fear of the LORD is the beginning of wisdom; all who follow his precepts have good understanding. To him belongs eternal praise" (Psalm 111:10).

Glory: "I am the LORD; that is my name! I will not yield my glory to another" (Isaiah 42:8).

Wisdom: "To the only wise God be glory forever through Jesus Christ! Amen" (Romans 16:27).

Thanks: "You … clothed me with gladness, to the end that *my* glory may sing praise to You and not be silent. O LORD my God, I will give thanks to You forever" (Psalm 30:11–12, NKJV).

Honor: "You are worthy, our Lord and God, to receive glory and honor and power, for you created all things, and by your will they were created and have their being" (Revelation 4:11).

Power: "His wisdom is profound, his power is vast" (Job 9:4).

Strength: "One thing God has spoken, two things I have heard: 'Power belongs to you, God, and with you, Lord, is unfailing love'" (Psalm 62:11–12).

Eternity: "Now to the King eternal, immortal, invisible, the only God, be honor and glory for ever and ever. Amen" (1 Timothy 1:17).

You can echo heaven's song right here on earth. Praise, glory, thanks, honor—these can be *your* offerings too. Wisdom, power, strength, and eternity—these are His, but He shares them with His children. Forever and ever. World without end. Amen and amen!

Dig a Little Deeper

- What does it mean to honor someone? Who do you honor with your time, your attention, your enthusiasm, your words, your support?

- Would it be easy to share something special that belongs only to you with someone else?

- Read 1 John 3:18–24. How does John urge us to live once we belong to God?

HEDGE OF PROTECTION

A Bible Lesson

Have you not put a hedge around him and his
household and everything he has? You have
blessed the work of his hands, so that his flocks
and herds are spread throughout the land.

—JOB 1:10

Place a hedge of protection around them." I often hear this
plea for supernatural support during prayer meetings. And
of course, we're not talking about a neat row of shrubbery. We
want God to surround a person with His angels, like watchmen
protecting a field that's valuable because it's ready for harvest.

Oddly enough, we're borrowing a phrase from Satan. In
the book of Job, he complained before the throne of God about
God's protection of Job.

We may never know just how often God has sheltered us
with a hedge. He and His angels surround us, hide us, and shield
us. He commands His angels to guard us, and so we are safe.

For You, O LORD, will bless the righteous; with favor You
will surround him as *with* a shield.

—PSALM 5:12 (NKJV)

You are my hiding place; you will protect me from trouble and surround me with songs of deliverance.

—PSALM 32:7

The LORD's unfailing love surrounds the one who trusts in him.

—PSALM 32:10

The angel of the LORD encamps around those who fear him, and he delivers them.

—PSALM 34:7

You have hedged me behind and before, and laid Your hand upon me.

—PSALM 139:5 (NKJV)

Dig a Little Deeper

- How do all these "hedge" verses encourage you?
- Read Psalm 139:5–10 (or the whole chapter). What held David in awe? How close did he feel to his Maker? Why was he overflowing with praise?

ENCAMPMENT OF ANGELS

Meeting an Angel

He struggled with the angel and won. Jacob
wept and begged for his blessing.

—HOSEA 12:4 (NIRV)

Jacob had wrestled both birthright and blessing from his brother Esau. At that time, he'd fled from his twin's hatred to the safe haven of Laban's household. His uncle had welcomed him with open arms. At first. For the blessing worked, and God's favor made Jacob flourish. His sons were many. His flocks were strong. His wealth surpassed that of his father-in-law and brothers-in-law. And Jacob saw in Laban's eyes the same distrust that had once burned in Esau's.

He would not wait to see if suspicion would turn to hatred.

Taking his wives, sons, and flocks, he left for home. It was impossible to cover the tracks of so large a company, so he wasn't surprised when Laban caught up. Anger. Injured feelings. Accusations. But the break was made clean by God's own meddling, for he'd warned Laban off in dreams.

Then God came to Laban the Aramean in a dream at
night and said to him, "Be careful not to say anything
to Jacob, either good or bad."

—GENESIS 31:24

Further proof of God's favor soon arrived. Jacob and his cattle, sheep, donkeys, goats, servants, and children reached a safe haven in the wilderness, with angels to meet them. "This is the camp of God!" he exclaimed, naming the place *Mahanaim* (Gen 32:1–2).

Within the heavenly encampment, Jacob made his plans. He dispatched messengers to Esau, sending word of his return. He fudged a few details. He flattered and fawned in his messages. He sent traveling parties in strategic intervals. And finally, he sent his own wives and sons across the Jabbok river, promising to follow in the morning.

Nightfall found him wrestling once more, and this time with one who was unlike any man or angel Jacob had met. Even with a wrenched hip, Jacob lived up to his name: grasper.

"You cannot defeat me."

"I won't give up!" countered Jacob.

"Enough." The angel pointed to the eastern sky. "Look, the sun is rising."

"I won't let go unless you bless me!"

"So be it." His opponent asked, "What is your name?"

"Jacob."

And then the angel said, "Not any longer. Your name is Israel."

"What's your name? Please tell me."

But Jacob—now Israel—did not receive an answer. But wasn't it enough to have encountered a messenger of God and lived? As the sun rose, he limped away with his blessing.

Dig a Little Deeper

- Jacob was bold in asking for a blessing. When would you be bold before God?
- What's the story behind your name or a nickname?
- Why did God give new names to some people (see Gen. 17:5–6; 32:28)?

THE HIDDEN DEEP

A Bible Lesson

Be alert and of sober mind ...
—1 PETER 5:8

The Bible talks about a spiritual war that rages unseen. Satan rebelled against God, and when he was cast out of heaven, a third of the angels fell with him (see Rev. 12:4). We're told that many of the old gods and idols that ancient people worshiped were actually demons (see Deut. 32:17). In other places in the Bible, fallen angels are referred to as "unclean spirits" (Acts 5:16 NKJV), "familiar spirits" (Lev. 20:6 NKJV), and "principalities" (Rom. 8:38 NKJV). In these same passages, the NIV uses "evil spirits" and warns against associating with mediums and spiritualists.

Not every fallen angel roves the earth looking for trouble. Many have been imprisoned. They're locked up until their judgment day arrives. You may run across references to *Tartarus*, one of the words translated as *hell* in our Bibles. This is a deep, dark place where demons have been chained away.

> God did not spare angels when they sinned, but sent them to hell, putting them in chains of darkness to be held for judgment.
>
> —2 PETER 2:4

> And the angels who did not keep their positions of authority but abandoned their proper dwelling—these he has kept in darkness, bound with everlasting chains for judgment on the great Day.
>
> —Jude 1:6

Demons are terrible, but fear not. In Romans 8:38–39, Paul declares, "For I am convinced that neither death nor life, neither angels nor demons, neither the present nor the future, nor any powers, neither height nor depth, nor anything else in all creation, will be able to separate us from the love of God that is in Christ Jesus our Lord."

Jesus told His disciples, "I am sending you out like sheep among wolves. Therefore be as shrewd as snakes and as innocent as doves" (Matt. 10:16). You need to know about your enemy, but don't let them fascinate you. Curiosity can lead you down dangerous paths. Paul said, "I want you to be wise about what is good, and innocent about what is evil" (Rom. 16:19). May this be true of you as well.

Dig a Little Deeper

- You've probably heard the saying, "curiosity killed the cat." What's the underlying warning? What does Jesus say in Luke 12:25–26 about worrying over things you can't control?

- How can you be wise about what is good and innocent about what is evil? When is this easier said than done?

DIVINE INTERVENTION
Meeting an Angel

All at once an angel touched him.
—1 KINGS 19:5

Elijah shouted his voice hoarse then ran his feet raw.

Only a fool made an enemy of royalty. Especially when the kingdom was under the heel of Queen Jezebel. Despite the miracles Elijah performed at Mount Carmel, the queen rebelled against the one true God. Her promise to steal his prophet's dignity, to tear screams from his throat, then to break him over the altar of a heathen god made Elijah's skin crawl.

With no sign of divine intervention in sight, his only hope of robbing her of this dark victory was to stay out of her clutches. He found the end of his strength in the middle of nowhere and collapsed under a broom tree. Pulling his knees to his chest, he hid has face with his cloak and wished for the oblivion of sleep.

Then he felt a hand on his shoulder. A firm shake.

Opening dull eyes, Elijah stared at the lone representative of heaven who knelt by his side. "What now? What next?" he asked wearily.

The angel's answer was short but kindly spoken. "Get up and eat."

Elijah was sorely tempted to turn his back. He didn't want food. He wanted a word from God ... a break ... a glimpse of what was in store ... or even some kind of reassurance that everything had been worthwhile. But the cake of bread stirred his stomach's interest.

He ate. He drank. And when the angel left him, Elijah retreated once more into sleep.

A second time, the angel touched him. "Get up and eat."

Elijah stared sullenly at the food and drink. Apparently, God wanted him to live. That was a small comfort.

Then the angel added, "The journey is too much for you."

The prophet's eyes watered at this acknowledgment. How could it be that the one who called down fire from heaven had come to this? He was a fragile vessel, and he trembled at the thought of being smashed to the ground.

Food.

Water.

Rest.

Company.

The angel filled the prophet's belly, quenched his thirst, watched over his slumber, and listened to his complaints. Eventually Elijah's strength returned. Then God led him to the field where Elisha, son of Shaphat awaited God's call.

Dig a Little Deeper

- When do you feel like you want to give up?
- When you're tired, hungry, or worried, how do you feel about your life? Can you relate to Elijah's distress?
- How important is friendship compared to food and water?

PRINCE OF DEMONS

A Bible Lesson

You once walked according to the course
of this world, according to the prince of
the power of the air, the spirit who now
works in the sons of disobedience.

—EPHESIANS 2:2 (NKJV)

Did you know that the devil is a prince? He has his fair share of nicknames, one of which is "the prince of the power of the air." It's a snazzy title. And a trifle irksome for those of us who don't like to give any honor to our oldest enemy. But the Bible isn't flattering Satan. In a sense, he really *does* have a kingdom of his own. Satan is called "the prince of demons" (Matt. 12:24) and the ruler of darkness (see Eph. 6:12). He's grasping at temporary glories, but his reign will end.

The true Prince will return, and His kingdom is everlasting. Jesus is called "Prince" (Acts 5:31), the "Prince of life" (Acts 3:15 NKJV), and the "Prince of Peace" (Isa. 9:6). Try as he might, the fallen angel of light cannot outshine the "light of the world" (John 8:12), "the bright Morning Star" (Rev. 22:16), the "rising sun … from heaven" (Luke 1:78).

Jesus can't be outdone.

Therefore God exalted him to the highest place and
gave him the name that is above every name, that at
the name of Jesus every knee should bow, in heaven

and on earth and under the earth, and every tongue acknowledge that Jesus Christ is Lord, to the glory of God the Father.

—PHILIPPIANS 2:9–11

The highest place. The greatest honor. Far better titles. Oodles more names and nicknames. Take the time to seek them out and learn them by heart. They teach us who Jesus is.

Dig a Little Deeper

- What nickname (and ultimate fate) is ascribed to Satan in John 16:11?
- Look up the following verses and jot down the nicknames for Jesus. These are only the beginning; there are dozens more!

  Isaiah 55:4

  Hebrews 4:14

  Luke 4:23

  John 3:2

  1 Timothy 4:10

  Mark 12:10

  Acts 10:42

  Daniel 7:9

  John 9:5

  Numbers 24:17

  Revelation 5:5

  Song of Songs 2:1

  Isaiah 9:6

Q. WHAT KIND OF ANGEL WAS SATAN?

Q&A

> One day the angels came to present themselves before the LORD, and Satan also came with them.
>
> —JOB 1:6

There's a descriptive passage from the prophet Ezekiel that seems to indicate that before Satan fell, he served God as one of the cherubim. It extols his beauty and perfection then recounts his pride, sin, and disgrace. God adorned him, anointed him, and ordained him, yet wickedness found his "guardian cherub."

> This is what the Sovereign LORD says: "You were the seal of perfection, full of wisdom and perfect in beauty. You were in Eden, the garden of God; every precious stone adorned you: carnelian, chrysolite and emerald, topaz, onyx and jasper, lapis lazuli, turquoise and beryl. Your settings and mountings were made of gold; on the day you were created they were prepared. You were anointed as a guardian cherub, for so I ordained you. You were on the holy mount of God; you walked among the fiery stones. You were blameless in your ways from the day you were created till wickedness was found in you. Through your widespread trade you were filled with violence, and you sinned. So I drove you in disgrace from the mount of God, and I expelled you, guardian cherub, from among the fiery

stones. Your heart became proud on account of your beauty, and you corrupted your wisdom because of your splendor. So I threw you to the earth; I made a spectacle of you before kings.

—Ezekiel 28:12–17

This "guardian cherub" was lavishly made. God's creativity can be seen in every detail. Beauty. Purity. Perfection. He was welcome in both God's throne room and in His garden. And yet Satan broke faith with his Creator and fell.

Dig a Little Deeper

- What did Satan have going for him?
- What do those verses hint at about God's feelings for His creation?
- What brought about Satan's downfall? What were the consequences? What's the warning for us?

SECURE THE TOMB
Meeting an Angel

There was a violent earthquake, for an angel of
the Lord came down from heaven and, going to
the tomb, rolled back the stone and sat on it.

—MATTHEW 28:2

Standing guard over a dead man," sighed one of the guards.
"He's not going anywhere."

"It's grave robbers we're guarding against. Not the dead.
Right, captain?" his cohort said.

The centurion, their leader, stirred enough to say, "Those
are our orders. But ... I wonder."

The second fellow wasn't ready to let things go. "Wonder
what, sir?"

"It's just ... I was there. When this man died, I was right
there," the centurion explained. "Did you feel the earthquake?"

"Everyone did. Rattled the whole city," the second guard
said.

The centurion's jaw tightened. "It was Him. He breathed
His last, and it was like ... the world broke apart. Made me think
the things His people believed had some truth to it."

"Yeah? What did they think?"

"They called Him the Son of God."

"A god?" snorted the first guard.

"*The* God," corrected the centurion. He flexed the hand
that had gripped the hammer he used to nail Jesus to the cross.

"These Jews believe there is only one God. And we killed Him. And He's coming back."

"Ridiculous! Dead is dead, and this guy's two days gone."

———————

Around sunrise, the guards jumped to their feet as the ground renewed its shaking.

Tossed to his hands and knees, the centurion struggled for composure. Scanning the area, he called to his two men. "You all right?"

A groan. A whimper.

That's when he realized that he could see more clearly, and not because of the distant glow on the eastern horizon. He rolled to his feet and brought up his weapon, but he made no further move. His men were down—fainted dead away, and a shining man broke the seal on the tomb.

Letting the point of his sword droop, the centurion said, "I'm supposed to stop you."

The angel's face was like lightning. His clothes were as white as snow. Ignoring the gaping centurion, he rolled aside the stone as if it were nothing.

He tried again. "You can't take the body."

The angel took a seat on the stone and calmly announced, "He is already gone. Jesus is risen, just as He said."

Dig a Little Deeper

- According to Mark 15:22–39, what did the centurion posted at the foot of the cross see and hear?

- If this man came to faith on that day, he wasn't the first. What happened in Matthew 8:5–13?

- What does Luke add to the centurion's story in Luke 23:47?

Q. HOW LONG HAVE PEOPLE KNOWN ABOUT ANGELS?

Q&A

> After he drove the man out, he placed on the
> east side of the Garden of Eden cherubim
> and a flaming sword flashing back and
> forth to guard the way to the tree of life.
>
> —GENESIS 3:24

From the very beginning. Perhaps the heavenly hosts were in attendance when God would join Adam in their evening walks through Eden (see Gen. 3:8). Maybe they were already coming and going by way of a heavenly staircase, serving God here on earth (see Gen. 28:12). It's possible, but the first *direct* mention of angels comes in the third chapter of Genesis, and not in the happiest of circumstances.

Eve is deceived, and Adam follows her into sin. Humanity falls, and sin takes hold of the world in manifold ways—thorns, weeds, disease, hardship, pain, predators, weeping, and death. Adam and Eve are suddenly on the outside, looking back at everything they've lost. And the way back is barred by cherubim and a flaming sword. Since *cherub* is singular and *cherubim* is plural, we know that there are at least two angels on guard. Adam and Eve could see them plainly.

> So the LORD God banished him from the Garden of Eden to work the ground from which he had been taken.
>
> —GENESIS 3:23

When I was a child, I used to think God was too harsh with Adam and Eve. Shouldn't they be able to say sorry and go back home? Curses and banishment seemed a terrible fate for two people who didn't mean to be bad. I longed to ease their burden by extending the same grace God gives to us. Why couldn't they have a second chance?

But I was far more shortsighted than God. Not until much later did I understand that casting Adam and Eve out of Eden was the first step in His plan to save them. They'd taken fruit from the Tree of the Knowledge of Good and Evil, even though God told them not to eat it. If Adam and Eve had eaten from the *second* tree in the garden—the Tree of Life—they would have been locked in a sinful state for all eternity. So God put them out with a promise that He was preparing a way back through their offspring (see Gen 3:15). When the time was right, sin and death would be defeated, and eternal life would belong to the children of God once more.

Dig a Little Deeper

- When do you most want a second chance? Can you think of a time when someone gave you that opportunity?
- What can an apology do? What can't an apology do? Why is there a difference?
- God's plan for redemption worked in our favor. What does Paul say about it in Ephesians 1:11–12?

TOLD YOU SO

Meeting an Angel

They came and told us that they had seen a
vision of angels, who said he was alive.

—LUKE 24:23

Mary hadn't slept in two days. Eyes scratchy, head aching, she clutched a small bundle of spices and perfume to her chest. Even in all of Friday's confusion, Nicodemus and Joseph of Arimathea had managed to dress Jesus' body in myrrh and aloes and a burial cloth.

Saturday had been spent pulling together shattered pieces. Peter was inconsolable. Judas was dead. John stuck close to their Lord's mother. James posted guards. Some had suggested going home or into hiding, but Mary had no desire to see Magdala again. Her heart rebelled against creeping into shadows as if she was ashamed. Wouldn't their leaving turn everything to nothing?

Mary had been dreading this morning. She'd stood by, shaking and shaken, when the men took down Jesus' battered and broken body. Now it was her turn. To anoint His body. To face His death. Could her faith survive this good-bye? Maybe not. She swallowed back tears even as the other Mary burst into fresh tears.

Wrapping her arm around her friend's shoulders, Mary Magdalene whispered, "Almost there, dear. Take courage."

If only she could follow her own advice. As they rounded the final bend, her stomach knotted. What business did the sun have, rising as if life could go on? Why did birds sing in mockery of her sorrow?

Salome saw it first and drew up short. "What's going on? Who rolled back the stone?"

"The soldiers?" Mary asked, her voice thick with dread.

The other women swapped worries. "Will they arrest us? What are they up to? Can they do this? Haven't they done enough?"

No stranger to trouble, Mary Magdalene took the lead. But instead of Roman guards, she found two strange men. And they seemed to have been waiting for her.

"Fear not!"

Yet she trembled. For these were angels.

"Jesus isn't here. He's risen, just as He said."

Just as He said? Was it possible? Words and phrases came to mind, and she echoed, "He told us. But I didn't want to believe Him."

"And now?" the second angel inquired.

Mary Magdalene could only nod. Heaven's messenger gestured to the wide open tomb, and she went to see for herself. Fears faded. Doubts died. Joy dawned.

Dig a Little Deeper

- What was Mary Magdalene afraid to face at the tomb?
- The words "just as He said" are similar to "told you so"? When are you glad to hear, "I told you so"?
- Think about the range of emotions Mary and the other women went through in that single morning. How did the day begin? What was the finale?

Q. HAVE YOU EVER SEEN AN ANGEL?

Q&A

Are not all angels ministering spirits sent to serve those who will inherit salvation?

—HEBREWS 1:14

Maybe. Several years ago, my husband and I took a Sunday afternoon drive out to one of the state parks along Lake Michigan. It was off-season, blustery, and the beach was virtually deserted. Only one other vehicle was in view—a small pickup farther along the beach, down by the shoreline. We watched the sun set over the water, then tried to turn the car around to head home. Moments later, our back wheels had slipped off the paved road and up to their hubcaps in fine sand.

There we sat—one distressed man, his very pregnant wife, and two small children strapped into their car seats. We were miles from anyone ... except for the two young men in that solitary pickup truck. They took our predicament as their cue. They had rope. They knew how to use it. They rescued us in our time of need. I've never been able to shake the idea that they were waiting for us. Maybe they were our angels.

Dig a Little Deeper

- When were you or someone you know helped by God in a miraculous way?

- The Bible encourages us to be kind to strangers. Why was this commandment established back in Exodus 23:9?

- Look at Luke 24:13–35. These travelers didn't realize what was happening until much later. How would you have felt in their shoes?

Neither Angels, Nor Demons

A Bible Lesson

Your will be done, on earth as it is in heaven.
—Matthew 6:10

You can't study the different Bible verses about angels without finding references to fallen angels. These demons are capable of terrible things, which can be scary to think about. They were cast from heaven to earth, which means they've been here for thousands of years. Hardly a comforting thought, but don't let God's enemies distract you from something else that's true.

No demon can come between you and God.
Neither can any angel, so fear not.
Nothing here and now can change this truth.
Nor will any future event.
Not the highest of heights.
Nor the deepest of depths.
Nothing in the created world.
Nothing in your life.
Not even death.

And if these promises have a familiar ring, that's good. Because Paul's words hold a promise you can hang onto. Let them convince you.

> For I am convinced that neither death nor life, neither
> angels nor demons, neither the present nor the future,
> nor any powers, neither height nor depth, nor anything
> else in all creation, will be able to separate us from the
> love of God that is in Christ Jesus our Lord.
>
> —ROMANS 8:38–39

Dig a Little Deeper

- What seems to come between you and the time you want to spend with God? What distracts you?
- What's the highest you've ever been? The lowest? The deepest? The happiest? The saddest?
- Why can't the truth ever be changed?

Q. CAN DEMONS DO WHATEVER THEY WANT?

Q&A

> Jesus healed many who had various diseases. He also drove out many demons, but he would not let the demons speak because they knew who he was.
>
> —MARK 1:34

Stories about angels inspire a sense of wonder. Winged warriors and radiant messengers. Shining servants of God who meet humans in times of need, carrying words that change lives. But not every angel remained faithful. Those who fell became our enemies. So should we be afraid of these demons? Can they harm us? Let me remind you of a few things.

Hedge of protection: God's word is absolute. Even the demons must obey, like the time Satan is summoned with the other angels in the book of Job. Job was a righteous man set up as an example, and Satan complained about it. "Have you not put a hedge around him and his household and everything he has?" (Job 1:10). Job was untouchable. Even when Satan was given the chance to shake Job's faith, God warned him not to lay a finger on the man. Job's life belonged to God.

Held in check: Jesus also demonstrates His authority over demon kind. They recognized Him and fled before Him. Jesus even prevented them from telling people who He was (see Mark 1:34).

Guide and guard: God is quite capable of keeping His children safe, even in dangerous situations. A good example of His watch-care is His action in Exodus: "See, I am sending an angel ahead of you to guard you along the way and to bring you to the place I have prepared" (Ex. 23:20). The psalmist also wrote, "For he will command his angels concerning you to guard you in all your ways" (Ps. 91:11).

The name of Jesus: The Bible indicates that the very name of Jesus can turn away the enemy. When Jesus sent out the seventy-two disciples, they returned with joy. "Lord, even the demons submit to us in your name" (Luke 10:17). And again, before Jesus returned to heaven, He prayed, "Holy Father, protect them by the power of your name, the name you gave me" (John 17:11).

In His hand. There's a good reason Christians sometimes refer to faith as "asking Jesus into our hearts." His Spirit joins us, making His home inside us (see 1 Cor. 3:16). He's the Holy Spirit of God "with whom you were sealed for the day of redemption" (Eph. 4:30). Your soul is safe, for "your life is now hidden with Christ in God" (Col. 3:3). The enemies of God can never touch that.

Should we be worried about demons meddling in our lives? No. Can Christians face hardships? Does bad stuff happen to good people? Will the going get tough? Yep. That's life. But believers are set apart. We bear His name. We're in His hand. His angels defend us. His enemies cannot cross any line He has drawn. So even if life gets crazy or confusing, don't forget that *nothing* can touch the part of you that's uniquely *you,* because you are God's. He has promised to keep your soul safe for all eternity.

Dig a Little Deeper

- Where are we safe (see Isa. 49:2)?

- What does Paul have to say on the matter in Ephesians 1:13–14? How does this calm any fears you may have had?

- Persecution and hardship are still very real. Consider Paul's words in 2 Corinthians 4:8–9. What is his attitude in the face of life's ups and downs?

Two Men

Meeting an Angel

"You will be my witnesses in Jerusalem, and in all Judea and Samaria, and to the ends of the earth." After he said this, he was taken up before their very eyes, and a cloud hid him from their sight.

—Acts 1:8–9

D on't go!"
Even after forty days of explanations, there were those who didn't want to be left behind. Thomas blinked back tears, but he didn't protest. He and the rest of the original twelve understood. Still, none of them could tear their eyes away from the sky. Which is probably why no one noticed the sudden arrival of two strangers.

A woman's startled cry sounded somewhere off to Thomas's left. People stumbled backward, and murmurs rippled outward.

"What is it?"

"What's happening?"

"Can you see?"

Thomas shouldered his way closer, ready to confront any troublemakers, but his righteous indignation vanished at the sight of heavenly raiment. Two men in shining clothes stood before them.

"Men of Galilee! Why do you stand here looking into the sky? This same Jesus, who has been taken from you into heaven, will come back in the same way you have seen him go into heaven."

Thomas wasn't sure if they'd just been comforted or scolded. Peter looked sheepish. James elbowed his younger brother. Martha linked arms with her siblings. In the midst of their awe, peace reigned. Everything was happening just as Jesus said it would.

As the crowd dispersed, they knew what to do next. Spread the word. Debunk the lies. Bear witness to the truth they'd seen with their own eyes and touched with their own hands. From here on out, believers would need greater faith than his.

> Because you have seen me, you have believed; blessed are those who have not seen and yet have believed.
>
> —JOHN 20:29

Dig a Little Deeper

- When is it hard to say good-bye?
- Read Acts 1:3. How long was Jesus with His disciples after the Resurrection? What did He accomplish during that time?
- What were the disciples prepared to do after Jesus went to heaven?

Q. WHEN CAN YOU TRUST AN ANGEL?

Q&A

> But even if we or an angel from heaven should preach a gospel other than the one we preached to you, let them be under God's curse!
>
> —GALATIANS 1:8

People will often say to me, "I wish I could meet my angel!" In these situations, my mind zips through a bunch of possible responses. Because I completely understand what they mean. But I'm not so sure *they* understand what it could mean for them. Angelic visitors usually leave their unwitting host or hostess with a mind-boggling message or dangerous mission.

And there's always a risk that a supernatural guest could be an angel of the fallen variety. After all, Jesus warns that the devil scatters weeds amidst the good seeds (see Matt. 13:38–39), and Paul warns that "Satan himself masquerades as an angel of light" (2 Cor. 11:14). Demons are capable of wonder-working, so miracles are no proof of faithfulness. And like their father before them, fallen angels are skilled flatterers and liars. So what does that leave?

Angels don't want your worship: In Revelation 22:9, God's angel is flustered by John's attempt to show him reverence. "Don't do that! I serve God, just as you do. I am God's servant, just like the other prophets. And I serve God along with all who obey the words of this book. Worship God!" (NIrV).

Angels will never contradict God: It's easy to believe someone who tells you what you want to hear. In fact, Paul warned, "The time will come when people will not put up with sound doctrine. Instead, to suit their own desires, they will gather around them a great number of teachers to say what their itching ears want to hear. They will turn their ears away from the truth and turn aside to myths" (2 Tim. 4:3–4). A true angel of God will never contradict God's Word.

Of course, that means you need to know your Bible pretty well if you're going to sniff out a liar!

Dig a Little Deeper

- Stuff can look good and sound good. How can you know when something *is* good?

- What does Jesus reveal about the devil in John 8:44?

- In Romans 16:17, what does Paul say to watch out for? How does this compare to Jesus' statement in Matthew 10:16?

THE FACE OF AN ANGEL

Meeting an Angel

All who were sitting in the Sanhedrin looked
intently at Stephen, and they saw that his
face was like the face of an angel.

—ACTS 6:15

Righteous indignation turned the members of the synagogue into a mob. As they hustled Stephen out of the city, Saul followed. This was his doing. And his duty.

As a Pharisee, he held the law in the highest esteem. That's why he couldn't turn a blind eye to the new heresy that had cropped up around the teachings of a radical. Saul had closely questioned neighbors and businessmen, and Stephen's reputation was excellent. But the man was some kind of miracle-worker. He did wonders in the name of Jesus, the so-called Christ.

"Why do they cling to hope? Their 'Messiah' is dead." Saul smirked. Thanks to Saul, Jesus' followers would meet the same end.

Tearing down a pillar of the community hadn't been easy. The synagogue had been forced to bring in outsiders. Jews from Cyrene and Cilicia. More from Asia and Alexandria. Once Saul had explained the danger Stephen posed to their community, they were more than happy to pick a fight. Saul's satisfaction dimmed slightly. Apparently, Stephen was so well spoken that two of his accusers had abandoned the synagogue to follow Christ.

"Unthinkable!" Saul snarled. This wasn't the first time he'd incited a stoning. Peer pressure was enough to seal Stephen's fate.

"Blasphemer!" called a member of the Sanhedrin. "Traitor!"

Rough shouts drowned out the protests of other Christians. Calls for reason found no willing ears. Accusers stepped forward. Their testimony stirred the crowd.

"You stiff-necked people, with uncircumcised hearts and ears! You are just like your fathers: You always resist the Holy Spirit!"

Enraged, they pushed Stephen into the rocky pit. Men shed cloaks, and Saul stood over them as the men of Jerusalem reached for stones.

Saul glared at the heretic, wanting Stephen to see his disdain. But the Christ-follower robbed him of all satisfaction. The man gazed steadily into the sky. "Look, I see heaven open and the Son of Man standing at the right hand of God." Stephen's last words brought a hail of stones.

"Lies," Saul muttered.

His words might have held more conviction if Stephen hadn't shined with the radiance of heaven. More than one person said it: "His face! It's like the face of an angel!"

Dig a Little Deeper

- Read Acts 22:3–5. Do you think Saul meant well? How can good intentions turn bad?
- When is stubbornness a good thing? When can it be dangerous?
- According to Acts 7:59–60, what were Stephen's final words? What's surprising about that? Why?

Q. Was Paul's thorn a fallen angel?

Q&A

> A thorn in the flesh was given to me, a
> messenger of Satan to buffet me.
>
> —2 Corinthians 12:7 (NKJV)

Most people agree that Paul's "thorn" was a physical handicap of some kind, but the apostle himself refers to it as a messenger of Satan and a tormentor (see 2 Cor. 12:7). That makes it tricky to piece together *exactly* what Paul's referring to in his letter to the Corinthians.

We know the apostle had his share of harrowing experiences—flogged, lashed, beaten, stoned, shipwrecked, and often toiling without food, water, sleep, and clothing (see 2 Cor. 11:23–27). And when he wasn't on the mend, he came down with other ailments. "Even though my illness was a trial to you, you did not treat me with contempt or scorn. Instead, you welcomed me as if I were an angel of God, as if I were Christ Jesus himself" (Gal. 4:14).

But it's interesting that right before Paul is given his "thorn in the flesh," he mentions a time when God caught him up into the spiritual realms.

> I know a man in Christ who fourteen years ago was
> caught up to the third heaven. Whether it was in the
> body or out of the body I do not know—God knows.

> And I know that this man … was caught up to paradise and heard inexpressible things, things that no one is permitted to tell.
>
> —2 CORINTHIANS 12:2–4

In this vision, Paul visited heaven, but unlike John's revelation, he was told *not* to share it with us. So we don't know if he saw angels, though it's possible. Afterward, Paul faced some kind of torment. Three times he asked God to take away his weakness. But God refused, saying, "My grace is sufficient for you, for my power is made perfect in weakness" (2 Cor. 12:9).

When it comes to any "thorn in the flesh," we can echo Paul's attitude: When we're weak, we can't be proud because we have to depend on God to carry us through.

Dig a Little Deeper

- According to 1 Corinthians 1:27, what does God choose to use? Why would He do that?
- What does Zechariah 12:8 say God will do for the weak one day?

SHOW ME THE WAY

Meeting an Angel

Now an angel of the Lord said to Philip,
"Go south to the road—the desert road—
that goes down from Jerusalem to Gaza."

—ACTS 8:26

"I have obeyed," Philip murmured, squinting at the empty landscape. "What else *could* I do?"

When the angel had appeared before him, Philip had collided with the ground so fast that he'd seen stars. Once he had collected himself enough to accept a hand up, he'd dared to take a longer look at his visitor. Who wouldn't? Angels dwelt in God's presence, and that's where his Lord had gone.

Philip hadn't seen an angel since Jesus was carried up into the clouds. But that day he'd been one of the crowd, as amazed as the next guy. Being singled out was humbling. Holding out his hands, Philip laughed at the way they still shook. "*Fear not*, he said. That was harder to do."

He'd been caught alone during prayer in the garden. And at the angel's command, he'd left without a word to his hosts. Now that his head was clearer, he was wishing his tongue had untied long enough for him to ask a few questions. "Like … where am I going? And why?"

"Take the desert road south out of Jerusalem. Walk and keep walking." Simple instructions, easily followed. But as the day wore on, Philip wondered at God's purposes. He assumed he'd know the *why* eventually. Preferably before the heat overcame what strength he had left.

As Philip scanned the barren landscape that lay between Jerusalem and Gaza, sunlight glinted off metal. He squinted through the shimmer of heat. "Not a mirage," he murmured, picking up his pace. This had to be it.

His heart leapt as the indistinct blur resolved itself into a chariot. Its driver had pulled to one side of the road. Fine horses. Expensive robes. Dark skin. The Ethiopian was so intent on the document he was studying, he didn't look up until Philip loomed over him.

The man's surprise couldn't have been greater than if he'd just come face to face with an angel from on high. Philip smiled and said, "Hello, stranger. Do you understand what you're reading?"

"How can I?" he replied, displaying a scroll. "Unless someone explains it to me."

At a glance, Philip recognized the passage as Scripture. This man was reading Isaiah. "I can," Philip offered.

Breaking into a wide smile, the Ethiopian said, "Speak on, friend."

Dig a Little Deeper

- Who was this foreigner (see Acts 8:27)? How would you respond to God's call to do something if He didn't tell you why?

- If called upon, could you be ready to share the gospel? What would it take for you to feel prepared?

- How did this desert meeting end (see Acts 8:39)? How might this change your perspective about random encounters with other people?

ROUNDABOUT VERSES
A Bible Lesson

Put on the full armor of God, so that you can
take your stand against the devil's schemes.
For our struggle is ... against the spiritual
forces of evil in the heavenly realms.

—EPHESIANS 6:11–12

Some verses have a way of standing out. They're catchy. They're quotable. They stick out, and they stick with us. But when it comes to Bible study, it's important to pay attention to roundabout verses. Think of it as studying a verse in its natural habitat.

When it comes to spiritual warfare, one of those dazzling passages is about the armor of God. Ephesians 6:10–20 is the full passage where this appears. Paul provides a handy checklist: belt, breastplate, combat boots, shield, helmet, sword. Knowing that we *have* spiritual armor is great. Being able to label all the pieces and parts—admirable! But why do we even need this stuff?

Let's slow down and look at those roundabout verses. What's Paul saying? Let's compare notes.

God is our strength: "Be strong in the Lord" (6:10). Remember, if we have any might, it comes from Him.

Take a stand: "Put on the full armor of God, so that you can take your stand" (6:11). God has provided everything we need to protect ourselves.

We have struggles: Against an enemy we can't even see. "For our struggle is not against flesh and blood" (6:12).

Defend yourself: With truth, righteousness, faith, salvation, and "your feet fitted with the readiness that comes from the gospel of peace" (6:15).

Arm yourself: The only weapon we need is "the sword of the Spirit, which is the word of God" (6:17). You can equip yourself by memorizing key passages.

Keep on praying: And not just once in a while, but "on all occasions with all kinds of prayers and requests" (6:18).

Consider others: Your alert attitude isn't for your sake alone. Paul invites us to pray for one another. "Pray also for me, that whenever I speak, words may be given me so that I will fearlessly make known the mystery of the gospel" (6:19).

Take courage: Even Paul wanted more boldness. "Pray that I may declare it fearlessly, as I should" (6:20).

Paul calls attention to an invisible enemy. And the checklist Christians so often memorize is surrounded by words of encouragement and a call to action. Take a stand. Keep praying. Consider others. Take courage because God is our strength.

Dig a Little Deeper

- If you dressed in your spiritual armor every day, how would it affect your life?

- Does knowing that struggles are normal make them any easier to face? Why or why not?

- What does arming yourself with the Bible mean? And would you say you're well-armed?

STORM AT SEA

Meeting an Angel

Last night an angel of the God to whom I belong and whom I serve stood beside me.

—ACTS 27:23

Paul doubted he'd ever get used to the bottom dropping out from under him. Twist and spin. Pitch and roll. He braced himself as best he could in the sloshing ship hold. For three days, their ship had been driven by a violent storm. Battered and bruised, all Paul could do was stay out of the crew's way while they hauled at the ropes and rudder.

For three days, they had no relief. Without sun or stars to guide them, they were hopelessly lost. He was amazed when the captain directed the crew to lash the hull. Would it be enough to hold the ship together? He worried when they tossed all their cargo and tackle overboard. They'd given up hope. It was enough to make Paul wish for a whale. "Jonah's fish surely gave the prophet a smoother ride than this."

"Fear not."

Paul squinted, then blinked several times. An angel stood beside him. Help couldn't have been more welcome.

The angel said, "You must stand trial, so God won't let you die here. You will reach Caesar in Rome, and God will be gracious to your companions. The lives of your shipmates will also be spared if they stay with you."

As soon as his heavenly messenger vanished, Paul struggled to the captain's side. He had to shout above the wind and the waves as he pled his case. "Keep up your courage, men! I have faith in God that what the angel said will happen. We will be saved!"

Paul believed the angel's promise. Even when they were still storm-driven on the fourteenth day. Even when they found themselves in strange surroundings. Even when it looked like they'd be dashed apart on the rocks. Even though they were half-starved and exhausted. Even when reaching land meant ramming their ship into a sandbar. Even though the passengers and crew had to salvage planks and swim for land.

In the end, 276 people survived the wreck, just as the angel had said. Just as God had promised.

Dig a Little Deeper

- When were other times that God acted against impossible odds?
- Did everything go smoothly after the angel delivered a message from God?
- If someone thought your faith was crazy, what would you do?

Q. DO ANGELS ESCORT PEOPLE TO HEAVEN AFTER THEY DIE?

Q&A

The time came when the beggar died and the angels carried him to Abraham's side.

—LUKE 16:22

The basis for this idea is found in the parable where Jesus compares the demise of a beggar to that of a rich man. He says that when the poor man died, angels carried him into heaven. Does this mean that everyone whose life reaches its end can expect an angelic escort? Let's check a few other passages about the move to heaven.

The chariot: One of the flashiest departures has to be that of Elijah, who didn't actually die. "Suddenly a chariot of fire and horses of fire appeared and separated the two of them, and Elijah went up to heaven in a whirlwind" (2 Kings 2:11). Since angels are sometimes referred to as chariots (see Ps. 68:17) and fiery creatures (see Ps. 104:4), angels probably played a part in ushering Elijah home.

The walk: The only other man to elude death was Enoch, who walked faithfully with God (see Gen. 5:24). We're told later in Hebrews 11:5, "By faith Enoch was taken from this life. ... 'He could not be found because God had taken him away.' ... he was commended as one who pleased God." So no angels here. It seems God himself escorted Enoch into glory.

The trumpet: Angels are definitely involved in Jesus' return. He will "send his angels with a loud trumpet call, and they will gather his elect from the four winds" (Matt. 24:31). So Jesus will be sending His angels to gather up the faithful.

The twinkling: Paul described Christ's victory over death: "In a flash, in the twinkling of an eye … the trumpet will sound, the dead will be raised imperishable, and we will be changed" (1 Cor. 15:52).

Both the fear of death and its sting will be banished. I think one reason why we don't have to be afraid is that we're not alone. God and His angels are directly involved in the transition from a believer's life on earth to life everlasting. Death can't lay a finger on us. Like Jesus said, "What I'm about to tell you is true. Whoever obeys my word will never die" (John 8:51 NIrV).

Dig a Little Deeper

- What victory did Jesus win according to 1 Corinthians 15:55–56?
- In 1 Thessalonians 4:13–14, what reminder does Paul offer to those whose loved ones have died?
- When we believe in God, why do we not have to be afraid of dying?

THE BELOVED DISCIPLE

Meeting an Angel

He made it known by sending his
angel to his servant John.

—REVELATION 1:1

John's closest friends had scattered to every corner of the earth. Exactly as their Lord had commanded. Years had passed since John had seen any of the original twelve disciples, and now he was an old man. There was no doubt that the others had gone on before him. Hadn't he been the youngest? It only made sense that his wait would be the longest.

Taking his time, John made the short trip to the sea's edge. He groaned softly as he lowered himself to his favorite seat, a stone facing the eastern horizon. "Today would be a good day for a reunion," he murmured. Smiling at his foolish impatience, John let his eyes drift shut as he lapsed into prayer. Jesus would come for him by and by. Hadn't He promised as much?

Peace settled around the old apostle, and small waves lapped at the island that was his prison. Patmos wasn't the ends of the earth, but it would see John's own end. Unless the angels on high were drawing breath for a trumpet blast. "I miss you," John whispered.

Then light assaulted his eyelids, and he flinched, covering his face. A voice boomed, "Write on a scroll what you see!" John turned to look, and heaven opened like a door before him. The angel said, "Come up here, and I will show you what must take place after this."

> Then I looked and heard the voice of many angels, numbering thousands upon thousands, and ten thousand times ten thousand. They encircled the throne and the living creatures and the elders.
>
> —REVELATION 5:11

> And I saw the seven angels who stand before God, and seven trumpets were given to them.
>
> —REVELATION 8:2

> Then I saw another mighty angel coming down from heaven. He was robed in a cloud, with a rainbow above his head; his face was like the sun, and his legs were like fiery pillars.
>
> —REVELATION 10:1

The beloved disciple wrote down the final message from Jesus: "Look, I am coming soon!" and again, "Yes, I am coming soon" (Rev. 22:7,12,20) And at that time, every eye will see Jesus and know the truth.

Dig a Little Deeper

- Are you looking forward to *soon*? What would you like to experience before then?
- Heaven means reunion with Jesus. How do you think it will feel to finally be in his presence?
- What might God do through you if you serve Him for a lifetime?

Threshold Series

Christa Kinde

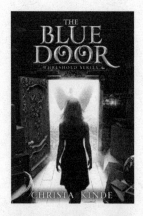

From author Christa Kinde, a supernatural series that introduces Prissie Pomeroy, a teen who discovers she can see what others cannot: angels all around.

Available in stores and online!